SPECTRUM OF LIES

BEFRIEND A ROGUE

BLUE FOX

OUTLANDERS OF THE MULTIVERSE COLLECTION

BY D.N. LEO

Narrative Land Publishing
Narrativeland.com

PART ONE

The course of true love never did run smooth.
A Midsummer Night's Dream , 1598
William Shakespeare

CHAPTER 1

The cold breezes seeped up from the ground, whirled into a small funnel, slashed at her skin, blew and tangled her beautiful long black hair. The gusts came from nowhere, carrying with them a strange chanting sound she didn't care for. It was the hovering sound of Hell—the sound of the dark magic. It was not supposed to follow her to the Daimon Gate, a universe far away from Earth. She had escaped from the haunt of the dark magic seventeen years ago, fleeing from a remote village in Ireland to London. She ran again a month ago, this time not by herself but with Lorcan, the love of her life, exiling themselves from Earth to the Daimon Gate. She assumed they had found their Heaven here.

Now she couldn't make it home—to the small castle Lorcan had named after her. She stood at the corner of a dead end street, beneath a gothic dome—a place Lorcan had told her several times not to take the short cut through. But she had taken this route several times in the last month. It was quiet and easy. It only took a few hundred yards around the corner, and she could go up the hill to their place. It should be perfectly safe based on what she was told.

The Daimon Gate was a virtuous universe— everything here was governed by righteousness. Orla couldn't help but roll her eyes when she thought about it. Being righteous was the very reason this whole universe was governed by machinery and a wicked computer system called the EYE. Only machines could tell right from wrong with no exception. It was perfectly normal for her, a human, to make mistakes, wasn't it? The fact that she wasn't good at following the rules was only a minor issue.

"All right, wallowing is a stupid thing to do, Orla," she muttered to herself. She had developed the strange habit of talking to herself since they had moved here. She didn't want to admit that it could be the result of loneliness and isolation. She shifted her stance and felt a tingling sensation on her toes and fingertips. It was just the chill, she thought, as she stared at a black brick wall in the place where she had seen her usual route home just a few seconds ago.

She had charged at it three times. When she stepped back, the path revealed itself; but when she approached, it closed up on her. Orla was certain if she turned around to go back to the main road, that path would close as well. In this universe, the physical rules were strange. She didn't understand them, nor did she appreciate them. She knew someone or something had to be playing a joke on her, and if this was a prank, it wasn't remotely funny. Her psychic ability was telling her nothing at the moment. Her palms were clammy and, even in the freezing air, a bead of sweat trickled down her forehead.

She shoved her right hand into her pocket to grab her cell phone and almost laughed at her own reflex. There were no such things as a cell phones here. In fact, the computer geniuses in the Daimon

Gate considered her earthly technology primitive. She merely wanted to call for help, but there was no time to fumble with the thing they used in place of a cell phone—a wrist unit. It was a funky type of watch to her, and a useless object that she had never bothered learned how to operate.

The wind grew stronger, and she thought she heard a howl echo from somewhere in the air. A dried tree branch on the ground flew up, whirled in the wind, and then aimed at her left arm, slashing into it.

"Oww," she yelped and grabbed at the cut. A small stream of blood oozed through the gaps between her fingers. A brick wall on her left cracked and collapsed. Orla just had enough time to jump out of its way. She turned around, glancing in the direction of the main road. A wall, coming from nowhere, slid across and blocked her view. She was being closed in. She turned back, looking at her usual corner path, open now. She made a small step forward, and the path closed up right in front of her.

She remembered what Lorcan had said—there were invisible networks of dimensional holes that only gatekeepers had access to and could control. She was sure these walls had come from those holes. More walls slid out from dimensional holes, surrounding her like a maze. A wall came in close proximity to where she stood and hit her from behind. Orla fell to the ground. She stood up immediately, her hands balled into fists. "That's enough, you coward. Wanna play with me? Show your pathetic face!" There was no response save for the sliding sound of black brick walls. Soon they would sandwich her, and she wasn't in the mood to be anyone's meal.

She swirled her palms in a circle as if making a ball out of thin air. A ball of fire formed. She smiled as if she couldn't believe what she had learned from her childhood had worked. She threw the fireball at the wall that blocked her way home. It crashed into the wall and burst into hundreds of pitiful fire particles. Another wall hit her from behind. Orla fell again onto the cold dirt road.

She stood up, created a bigger fireball, and hurled it at the wall. Again and again, she threw them. The sound of the balls hitting the walls was as loud as thunder. The wall cracked and shattered into a pile of dirt and then vanished. The cold wind still whirled, but it was not the icy breeze sending the chill to her spine right now.

A clapping sound came from a dark corner, followed by a man. He looked like a dark prince Orla had read about in gothic novels—tall with slightly long black hair framing a sinfully handsome face. His clapping and his smile sent a chill from her spine to her brain. Her blood ran cold. She had no idea who he was, but she had a feeling that he didn't come here to see her performance. He came to see her death.

CHAPTER 2

Orla pasted a smile on her face.

"Impressive," the man said. "It took a considerable amount of time and effort on my end to get to witness your dark magic." A faint accent penetrated his voice, but Orla couldn't make any sense of it.

"There was no dark magic. Just a trick to fool kids who still believe in Santa Claus." Orla stepped backward slightly, sizing up the man. He was at least as tall as Lorcan, so he had a height advantage over her. He seemed as agile as a cat with movements of an experienced fighter. It was obvious now that he controlled the walls that blocked her way home, and that meant he was a gatekeeper. Taking all that into account, Orla wagered that her chance of winning this fight was nonexistent.

"Who are you? And what do you want?" Orla asked.

"I am a gatekeeper."

"I figured as much. I can tell that by the way you're playing with the dimensional holes. But being a gatekeeper doesn't guarantee your safety when harassing an ordinary citizen like me. I'll report you."

The man chuckled. "I was only trying to protect the gate from intruders—and from those who cheated their way in."

Now her blood ran ice cold. The only person who knew Lorcan had cheated the system for them to come to the Daimon Gate was Ciaran LeBlanc. But Ciaran had promised not to tell anyone. Lorcan had never told the authority of the Daimon Gate that Orla was a trained sorceress who had used dark magic to cheat his life back, not once but twice. In this universe, if they were caught cheating the system for personal gains, they could face the death penalty.

"I don't know what you mean. But at the moment, as far as I'm concerned, you're harassing me."

"Let's cut to the chase. I don't have much time, and I don't think you and your lover have much time, either. You used the dark magic to throw fireballs at my walls. That's evidence of using it inside the Daimon Gate. I don't need to explain the consequences of that to you, do I?"

Orla shrugged. "Well, if it's in the system, we'll have to face the consequences. Usually, there's no way out of a severe penalty. So what's your ulterior motive for giving us a solution?"

The man laughed. "If all the people from Earth are as smart as you are, I could be in trouble." The man smirked. "Lucky for me, there aren't many of those around here. Yes, the evidence of your magic was captured within my system. At the moment, it's internal and under my control. That explains the number of walls I had to use to shield the view of the EYE. But I can report the evidence to central at any time—unless you do one simple thing for me."

"And what would that 'simple' thing be?"

"Ciaran LeBlanc used the system within your castle to cheat the system. I want you to get your man to report Ciaran to the central." His voice was as smooth and calm as still water. He locked his gaze with Orla.

"Ciaran LeBlanc, the king of Eudaiz?"

The man sneered. "Not for long."

"Why? Who are you? What did he do to you?"

"Come on. You don't owe him anything. But you owe your life to yourself. And don't you want to live happily ever after with your lover at your castle?"

Orla nodded. "I suppose so. But what if the council has already recorded my use of magic? If that's the case, I don't have to do anything you ask."

The man laughed. "Aren't you a skeptic?"

"I'd call it brain power."

"Right." The man approached Orla. "I'm not a big-time gatekeeper, but I can assure you, I am in total control of my limited world inside these walls. Each gatekeeper has a private zone into which even the EYE cannot intrude."

Orla arched an eyebrow, then as quick as lightning, she threw a fireball right into the man's chest. Taken off-guard, he staggered back, grunting in pain. Orla smiled. She might not have any physical advantage over this man, but she refused to go down easily. "If that's the case, then nobody will see me kill you," Orla said under her breath, hurling another ball. He dodged it and threw his dagger at her. She threw a ball at his hand, but missed.

As the wall behind him moved, the man was distracted. Seizing the opportunity, Orla threw another ball. The man dodged her fireball once again, and it sailed past him toward the wall behind him that had slid open.

Lorcan stood at the opening wall, holding a portable device. He ducked as the fireball flew past, missing his face by inches. The man waved his arm. Orla couldn't see anything except Lorcan yelling and pointing at her, and then the wall behind her hit her head. She slumped to the ground, and the whole world turned into darkness.

***

A large, gothic-looking arch stared down at her, making her blood run cold. There was something wrong with the air around them—her skin felt charged, almost like she was conducting electricity. Lorcan stood in the center of the arch, dancing away from the lightning bolts chasing him. Orla couldn't believe how many of them there were! There had to be at least a few thousand. She stood there, rooted to the spot, unable to help her lover. She kept trying to run out to help him, but he yelled at her to stay away and save herself. As he shouted at her, he stopped moving, just for half a second, barely escaping the next lightning bolt. Fighting her way free from whatever was holding her prisoner, she started to run to Lorcan, not heeding his warnings to stay away. She was getting frustrated because no matter how fast she ran, she didn't seem to be getting any closer. Tears started streaming down her cheeks as the hopelessness of the situation started to sink in. She watched helplessly as one of the lightning bolts hit Lorcan, causing him to burst into flame like a Roman candle. As his ashes fell into a neat little pile, Orla screamed in agony. Her heart was dying along with him.

***

"Orla! Orla! Come on, honey, you need to wake up now." Lorcan was trying to shake Orla awake, but so far it wasn't working. He had seen a gigantic wall hit her from behind, and then the man that she seemed to be fighting with fled the scene. He didn't understand why this was happening. The Daimon Gate was supposed to be the safest place for them, a self-contained world that was the entrance between universes. Who was the man she had been fighting with? He looked like a gatekeeper. Lorcan wanted to look the man up on his computer system, but at the moment, he couldn't leave Orla.

"Orla! Come on, baby, wake up for me now, okay?" He went back to shaking her gently, hoping she would open her eyes. Her eyelids fluttered, and she groaned. He swept her up in a tight embrace.

"What happened?" she asked groggily.

"I should ask you that."

She blinked, and then the encounter with the man came back to her. "We're in serious trouble, Lorcan," she said.

CHAPTER 3

Lorcan helped Orla sit up, leaning her against the head of the bed, then he went to get her some water. While Orla took tentative sips and looked at him over the rim of the glass, Lorcan sat at the side of the bed and checked the cut on her arm that he had secured with a bandage. He tried not to look into her eyes because all he saw in them was the trouble that would put to an end the short happy month they'd been living in the Daimon Gate. "What kind of trouble are we in, Orla? Who was the gatekeeper you fought with?" he asked when he thought any further delay on his part would seem odd to her. She told him about the man's demands. Lorcan said nothing for a long moment. He went to the window and stared silently outside. After a while, he turned to her. "You'd agree with me that we won't report Ciaran?"

"Of course. There's a dark side to Ciaran, and he must have created a lot of enemies along the way because of that, but he's an important man. People in his universe—their lives—depend on him. If we did anything to harm him, we wouldn't find a place in Hell."

The sorrow in Orla's eyes cut at Lorcan's heart. He wondered whether the universe Ciaran was ruling, the Daimon Gate, Earth, and anywhere else that had living creatures shared the same Hell. He had seen Hell on Earth when they fought to bring Riley back and tried to free Riley's late wife, Michelle. If he and Orla committed a sin now, would they return to that same Hell? Or did Daimon Gate have its own version of Hell?

"Lorcan!"

"Huh?"

He knew Orla was lonely in the Daimon Gate. They didn't have many friends here, and after what had happened to them on Earth, they didn't make friends easily. It had been a month, and the only time he'd seen the light back in her eyes was a couple of weeks ago when they'd had visitors. Ciaran LeBlanc and his people had stopped by on their way through the gate on a multiversal secret mission that he wouldn't talk about. Some creature had used dark magic on Ciaran, and Lorcan and Orla had done what they could to help him find out what it was. Orla had used her sorcery combined with Lorcan's computer skills, and for a little while, she had looked happy again. She'd been intrigued and had felt almost like she'd been back at her job on Earth.

They didn't, however, help Ciaran solely out of the goodness of their hearts. Ciaran made it clear that he knew that Lorcan had died on the 46th floor of the century tower, and that Orla had brought him back with her own dark magic, using it to cheat Lorcan back to life. He had used that as blackmail, and he'd also appealed to their sense of justice. Ciaran was to rule Eudaiz, a universe with hundreds of billion people who relied on him for their safety. Those two things combined had won them both over, and there was nothing else they could do but help him.

The Daimon Gate was a universe full of virtue— governed by virtuous people and operating on virtuous principles. The most serious crime in the universe was cheating any system for personal gain. Lorcan had passed the test that they'd given him and then demanded a deal to get Orla to come with him. The fact that Lorcan had cheated death and come back would be a grave offense, and considered cheating, because he might not be the same person who had initially passed the test. He also hadn't told them Orla's real identity, or the fact that she was a trained sorceress. That was something else that could be considered cheating the system. Lorcan's crimes were grave indeed, but no one knew about them yet. If Ciaran told anyone, then Lorcan would face death by a thousand lightning bolts. That was the vision Orla had just gotten in her delirium.

Ciaran had promised not to reveal their secrets to the Host of the Daimon Gate, and they trusted him. On the other hand, although Ciaran was the king of Eudaiz, if he traveled in the Daimon Gate, he had to play by their rules. If he got caught cheating the Daimon Gate system, he would be killed before he returned to his world. And Ciaran had cheated the system here, right in this castle. He did it to save a senior gatekeeper of the Daimon Gate, Brandon, the prince of the Red Castle. Brandon committed a crime and was supposed to die, but for some reason unbeknown to Lorcan, Ciaran had manipulated the computer system to change the sentence from death to demotion. If Lorcan reported that incident to the authority of the Daimon Gate, the next time Ciaran traveled via the gate, he would be killed.

"Do you think the EYE recorded my use of magic?" Orla asked.

Lorcan shook his head. "I don't think so. The gatekeeper you fought had blocked the signals well enough. But why did he want to expose Ciaran? The only reason I can think of is that someone is opposed to the fact that Ciaran saved the prince and the princess. But I would imagine there are many other ways to harm Ciaran. Why this way? And why would a gatekeeper of the Daimon Gate want to harm the king of Eudaiz?" he questioned.

Lorcan's wrist unit beeped. Text had come across the screen suggesting the call was made from the Host residence, asking Lorcan to come and meet with the Host of the Daimon Gate. His nerves started to heighten his senses, and he began to sweat.

He showed Orla the text. A soon as she saw the text, a tear rolled down her face. "The bastard has reported us!" she said.

CHAPTER 4

Virtue is the core value of the Daimon Gate. As the Host of the Daimon Gate, this man had to be the most virtuous man in the Cosmo, Lorcan thought. Given that, the Host wouldn't tolerate cheating from anyone. Lorcan shook his head, trying not to think about what may lie ahead of them. There were nine thousand gatekeepers at work here—why would this one want to cause them trouble? He asked Orla to stay in their bed chamber and he made a beeline toward the control room.

The Host only dealt with high-level executives within the gate and top-level executives from the participating worlds. No one knew who the Host really was, though rumor had it that he was once human and used to live on Earth. Lorcan was nervous. He answered the call, and almost instantaneously, a hologram appeared. The image was life-sized, and the man looked like a kindly old grandfather in his late sixties. He had a British accent, and it made Lorcan wonder if the two might have been neighbors at one point.

"Lorcan?" Before the Host could speak, Orla poked her head into the room. She saw the hologram in front of her, and her mouth dropped open. Not very many people had the honor of meeting the Host, for security reasons, but now that the two of them were seeing him in the hologram, they were a little starstruck. Lorcan excused himself hurriedly to the Host, rushed over to Orla, and ushered her outside.

"I'll be with you in just a second, okay honey? I don't think the Host would care for you to see him." She nodded and sat in a chair, clutching her stomach. Lorcan returned to the control room. The holocast of the Host stood in a beam of light, waiting. It had taken Lorcan a good two weeks to adjust to this universe's way of communication. A holocast was like a telephone on Earth, but the technology was a lot more advanced. The significant difference was not only the life-sized hologram, but the fact that the person could choose to step out of the light beam and enter the environment of the person he was speaking to.

"Lorcan, how are you and Orla faring? Have you had a chance to settle in properly?" The soft British accent calmed Lorcan's nerves a bit, but he still felt a chill in anticipation of what was coming. The Host wouldn't drop by his place simply for a cup of tea.

"We're doing fine. Sometimes it gets a bit lonely for Orla, but we're managing. I've made some progress with the project. Would you like a report now?"

"Lorcan, I'm going to speak to you off the record now. Whatever you say will be between us only. No record of it will appear anywhere or be recorded." The hologram of the Host took a few steps forward until he was completely out of the beam of light. His fuzzy edges solidified, and his unintelligible details became concrete. Something about him looked familiar, but then again, it could just be that he had one of those kindly old man faces. "Is there anything you want to tell me off the record before I tell you the reason I am here?"

Lorcan contemplated and then shook his head. He didn't think he was breathing, but he must have been. No one could hold their breath for that long. He swore he could hear the sound of a clock ticking, even though time in the Daimon Gate was different compare to Earth, and they didn't use clocks. It must be the countdown of his life he was hearing.

"Let me give you a hint. The EYE reports a glitch coming from your system here a couple of weeks ago, resulting in inconsistencies. Any idea what might have caused the problem?"

Lorcan felt as though the floor under his feet was shifting. He cleared his throat. "I don't know. What sort of problem? I sent out a lot of signals daily while working on your project."

The Host nodded. "That's how I figured out there was an inconsistency. I'm taking a preemptive step here. The computer hasn't reported the issue to the council. But soon, the tech department at central will put a report together, and the issue will be picked up. Are you sure you didn't do anything different?"

Lorcan matched the Host's gaze. "No. Nothing. If the EYE picked up discrepancies, please let me know, and I will formally address it."

The Host smiled. "You're a good man, Lorcan. It wasn't a mistake recruiting you. Thank you for protecting the person who sent out the discrepancies from your system."

Lorcan shoved his hands into his pockets and remained silent.

"The EYE can't record private conversation, Lorcan, you know that."

Lorcan nodded. "It seems you've fixed the discrepancies and know who caused them, so why are you telling me?"

The Host sat. "While I was looking into that particular issue, I came across a nuance, a piece of information from a computer database on Earth that recorded something about you and what happened at Century tower."

Lorcan whirled around. "How is that possible? The EYE can't see into private places."

"I said the information is from an *Earth* database."

"But it was recorded into the LeBlanc security system. It's not possible for an outsider to . . ." Then the truth dawned on him, and Lorcan gasped. "You . . ."

The Host smiled. "You did Ciaran a favor, so I will return the gesture, and I hope you appreciate it. I am Ciaran's father, so of course I have access to the LeBlanc's security system. That information alone is a life and death matter for many people.

Although Ciaran didn't expose you and Orla, the information *was* recorded. Sooner or later, it will leak."

"It already has, I'm afraid."

"I beg your pardon?"

"My wife was attacked by a gatekeeper just before your holocast. He forced her to use her magic and threatened to report us if we don't expose Ciaran."

"A gatekeeper?"

Lorcan nodded. "But I don't know who he is or his ulterior motive." Lorcan's hands were clenched into fists.

"How did he attack Orla?"

"He pulled his gatekeeper's walls from dimensional holes."

"He used his resources. There will be a record. I'll find out who he is. But that can't be good for you. When he has to answer to the incident, he will reveal your information."

Lorcan was pacing now, his face clouded over, his eyes stormy. He kicked an empty chair in frustration, sending it through the row of other chairs and creating quite a mess. The Host smiled calmly. "I would never come to you with an unsolvable problem. I appreciate your keeping your promise to Ciaran. So I have a suggested solution."

Lorcan stopped pacing. He shoved his hands into his pockets and stared at the Host, waiting for him to continue.

"There is an artifact, a key that we lost. It is the key to the life force of one of our gatekeepers. A long time ago, an unknown creature from another universe attacked the gatekeeper of Gate 131. The Daimon Gate connects to nine thousand portals, and this particular portal is an Eastern gate. The creature trapped the life force of the gatekeeper inside of a rock with the key of Psuche, locked the gate with the same key, then fled. No one can travel through that gate, and the gatekeeper can neither die naturally nor be saved. As to the creature's whereabouts, or even what it is, we have no further information. If you can obtain the key of the Psuche of Gate 131, it will solve your problem."

"How so?"

"Although I don't understand magic, and I am not a true believer, there is no rule set in stone saying you cannot use unexplainable resources in the Daimon Gate. The problem is that you have to report it and get it approved. The Eastern gate is a perfect example. That gatekeeper used to be a wizard on Earth."

Lorcan cocked an eyebrow.

"Yes, you heard me right. It was long before my time. Because of the gatekeeper's origin, it is deemed appropriate that you would recruit someone with expertise such as Orla's. I can put your case to the council, stating that I was aware of Orla's talent before I recruited you, and that you are now both recruited for the mission."

"You would lie to the council for me? I . . . I thought . . ."

"That I have to be the most virtuous man in the Cosmo? Well, I suppose I am. And I'm not lying. I will simply move the time I received the information about Orla up a little earlier." The Host smiled.

Lorcan ruffled his hair. "Thank you. I'll get you the key."

"It's not going to be a walk in the park. If it were, it could have been done long time ago."

Lorcan nodded. "I see. Thank you very much. I appreciate this."

The Host nodded and turned on the holocast beam. "I should return to my residence for tea." He smiled gently, like a grandfather, and turned on his heel, vanishing into the light beam.

CHAPTER 5

Orla had waited a few minutes to make sure the holocast was gone before she entered the control room and strode toward Lorcan.

"You were eavesdropping?" Lorcan cocked an eyebrow at her.

Orla shrugged, put her arms around him, and snuggled into his chest. Then she rose up on tiptoes to kiss him. She had no idea how they were going to find this unknown creature, but she knew that if anyone could do the impossible, it would be Lorcan. She was going to make sure that she was there with him. They did everything together, and she wasn't going to take a backseat and just watch his next adventure from the sidelines.

When he had regained his footing after the bone-melting kiss, Lorcan combed his fingers through her long black hair and kissed her forehead. "I guess you want to work on this with me?"

"Are you saying I'd never love you without having an ulterior motive?"

He smiled. "No and no. You always love me, the same way I love you. And that's unconditional. And you *always* have an ulterior motive for anything you do, irrespective of whether love is involved."

Orla pressed her body against Lorcan's and pushed him against the wall. "Well, this has no motive whatsoever." She slid her hands underneath his shirt and up his torso. Lorcan grabbed her. He kissed her jaw, trailing his kisses down her neck, rubbing against her smooth milky skin. He turned her around, pressing her against the wall. While his mouth was busy on her lips, his hands fumbled with the buttons of her blouse. She removed his shirt in one swift move, but Lorcan was unable to take hers off, fumbling again and ultimately yanking it open, tearing off all the buttons.

It was unusual of him, Orla thought. He knew every seam of her clothes, every zipper, button, and what-goes-where of a woman's dress. Sometimes Orla wondered how and where he got that knowledge.

Lorcan stopped. He looked at the buttons rolling across the floor. He then pulled her again into his arms and pressed his forehead against the wall. "I'm sorry," he whispered. "I'm out of my depth this time, Orla. I'm going to do my best to save us, but if I can't, I want you to get yourself out of here, do you hear me?" He had her face in his hands now, and they were standing forehead to forehead. She pushed him away.

"I saved your ass twice on Earth, and you think I'm useless now?"

"No. But you heard the Host. If it's doable, why hasn't anyone done it before? I can dig and find any data we need. I can fight. I can even kill. But magic! I don't even know where to start with that."

"Isn't that the very reason you'll need me? And if I'm not mistaken, I'm officially recruited in the mission, too. Do you seriously think I'm going to sit here and let you go on with this alone? And if we don't know anything about this creature, then you're going to need me there to help you find it!" The more she said, the angrier she became, and the higher in pitch her voice rose. Lorcan did his best to catch her fists as she angrily enunciated her little speech with them.

"Orla, I don't want you to get caught up in this. If I don't know what I'm doing, I can't let you go with me. It's dangerous." His voice was calm and neutral, but she knew that he was just letting her blow her steam off. She started crying, and he pulled her in close.

"If it's going to be as dangerous as you let on, then I'm not going to let you do it by yourself. You need me, and I need you. Please don't make me stay behind and worry about you. I want to come with you." When he saw the tears in her eyes, his voice became more soothing.

"All right. If that's what you want, then you can go with me. I don't want to be separated from you, either. But promise me if I fail, you'll go back to Earth and find my family. They will protect you because you are mine."

"I won't let you fail." They stood there in the middle of the control room, holding each other for countless minutes.

CHAPTER 6

It was as dark and creepy as it could be inside the Daimon Gate. Lorcan approached Gate 131 with caution, pushing Orla behind him. He wasn't sure if coming here was a good idea, but they had to start somewhere. The aura of the area made it easy to imagine zombies lurking just around the corner. It wouldn't have surprised him to see bizarre-looking creatures darting at them from seemingly nowhere. This wasn't exactly a gate. Perhaps it hadn't been in operation for a long time. There was no door, no lights, no computer, and no sign of living creatures.

The dark Gothic archway peered down at them, imposing and full of secrets. "This is used to be a gate, I think," Lorcan speculated.

Orla rubbed her hand along the wall, finding it damp as if it was perspiring. At the corner of the wall, her hand hit something lumpy. She moved closer to take a look, and the wall opened its eyes and blinked, sending her yelping leaping feet away from the wall. Lorcan darted to her, pushing her behind him. These weren't the wall's eyes—they were the eyes on an ancient man's face which was buried in the wall. Orla missed her weapons, the convenience of the rather violent devices she used to have on Earth. They would come in handy right now, she thought. She wagered Lorcan must have thought the same.

Lacking anything remotely threatening, Lorcan pointed his electronic notebook at the eyes of the man. "Don't move," Lorcan demanded, and then realized that was a stupid command—the man couldn't move. He was immobilized within the wall. Lorcan's eyes then widened as he came to a realization. "You were the gatekeeper!"

"He would smile and nod if he could," Orla commented as she had come to the same conclusion as Lorcan. "It must has been a long time since he's seen anyone. You think he speaks English?"

"Only one way to find out," Lorcan muttered. "Do you speak English? Please blink your eyes if you do."

The eyes blinked.

"We're going to find the key of Psuche to free you. Do you have any idea who took it or where it would be? Please blink for yes."

No blinking this time. Orla sighed. Lorcan paced, contemplating the possibilities. "I'm guessing each gate has its own unique key, am I correct?"

The eyes blinked. Lorcan nodded, a wave of energy rushing through him as he felt they were making progress. "You were a wizard before you became the gatekeeper?"

Blinks.

"Among nine thousand gates and nine thousand unique keys, the creature chose this particular gate and this particular key. Why?" Lorcan mumbled to himself. "The key has something to do with where you came from?"

There was no blinking.

"The key has something to do with you being a wizard?"

There was no blinking. Lorcan raked his hand through his hair. Orla approached. "Someone killed for the key, so it must be very important," Orla commented. The eyes blink rapidly.

Lorcan opened his electronic notebook. His fingers flew on the keyboard. He typed and typed, then paused, shaking his head, and resumed typing. In a short moment, Lorcan looked up and said, "The data suggests that there was a change of the gate key before your time. You were recruited to guard this gate and this key because of your magic. Does the key have anything to do with supernatural forces?"

The eyes blinked rapidly.

"Whoever got the key, can that person control the universes?"

There was no blinking.

"What about one particular universe?" The eyes blinked. Lorcan raised an eyebrow. "Eudaiz?" There was no reaction. "Xiilok?" There was no reaction again as Lorcan went through the list of universes connected to the Daimon Gate. The list was long, and there had been no further reaction from the eyes. Orla was pacing impatiently.

"Earth?" asked Lorcan.

Then eyes blinked rapidly. Sensing it, Orla whirled around. "Earth. Our friendly bloody Earth," she whispered.

Lorcan cleared his throat. "We might need to narrow things down a little bit. The Earth is quite large to look around aimlessly. Now this is the Eastern gate, so I guess I can safely narrow it down to the Eastern countries," he mumbled to himself, searching further on his notebook. Then his eyes sparked. "You're from Japan. Whoever took the key, he's from Japan as well?"

The eyes blinked rapidly. "So he stole the key to control Japan?" Orla deduced.

"Hey, don't roll your eyes. We're trying to help you here," Lorcan scolded.

"They stole the key to control the supernatural forces in Japan?" The eyes rolled again. Orla put her hands on her hips. "The mode of communication is that you blink your eyes to confirm a positive answer. Rolling your eyes is not acceptable. Keep doing that, and we'll leave you here to rot."

Lorcan lowered his voice so that he sounded calm. "So the key is in Japan now?"

The eyes blinked.

"Is that all you know?"

The eyes blinked again then drooped.

Lorcan waved his arms in the air. "Right. Japan it is. Not as bad as searching the entire Earth!"

They heard a *whoosh*. Orla's psychic ability had urged her to move just an instant before the arrow hit, so it only scraped her left arm. Lorcan charged in the general direction of the arrow's origination. Then all Orla heard were the sounds of men grunting and of kicks and punches hitting their target. Soon Lorcan emerged, dragging the man who had attacked her earlier. He was barely conscious. Lorcan continued to pound on the man. Whatever frustration he couldn't vent in the painstaking process of extracting information about the key from the entombed gatekeeper, he took out on this gatekeeper.

Orla pulled Lorcan back. "You'll kill him, Lorcan."

He gave the man a last kick before Orla pulled him out of reach of the man. "Scumbag," Lorcan snarled.

Lying on the ground, then man chuckled. "Yes, indeed I am a scumbag. But I'm alive. If you think you can use the Host against me, you're mistaken. I haven't done anything wrong, but you have. Now he's lied for you—he won't last long, Host or not."

"What the fuck are you talking about?"

"What I asked you to do wouldn't cost you anything. Giving Ciaran up is not going to end your world, but reporting me to the Host and getting him to back you will end both your world and his."

The man pulled himself up onto his knees.

"Who are you?" Orla asked.

The man smirked. "You don't need to know who I am. I gave you options. I asked you to do a very simple thing for me, but you didn't. You chose to go against me, and you helped a stranger like Ciaran LeBlanc. Now, no one is going to help you." Then in front of Lorcan and Orla, he surged up, ran at the buried gatekeeper, aimed his crossbow between the eyes, and shot. The eyes of the buried gatekeeper flared up, glassed over, and then vanished. Lorcan snarled and charged at the man, but he swung open a gatekeeper's dimensional hole, dove in, and disappeared. Lorcan didn't bother giving chase. He pulled out his handkerchief and took care of the cut on Orla's arm.

CHAPTER 7

As soon as they entered the hallway of their castle, they could see the lights from the control room and hear the signals echoing down the corridor. The robots announced that they had visitors and the visitors would like to see both of them. "Sure, so we're guests in our own home now," Orla remarked. Lorcan's jaw clenched, and his striking blue eyes darkened. He knew this was serious.

In the control room, they found the holocast of three members of the Daimon Gate council, one of them the Host. One of the other two was a tall creature with a human shape but an alien face.

There was no way for Lorcan and Orla to adjust to the appearance of the person from their earthly aesthetic standards. When the man spoke, streams of text translation in English floated in the air in front of him. The other member was a man in his late sixties who spoke with a New York accent.

"I'm sorry to intrude on your private space again. Since we last spoke, something happened in the council, and we need you to clarify some information," the Host said, his eyes locked with Lorcan's. Lorcan knew that was a warning sign.

He cleared his throat. "Sure. I'll give you as much information as I know. But before we start, I'd like to let you know that the gatekeeper at Gate 131 was killed just now. The information will be ready for you at central when you return."

"Killed? By whom?" the Host asked.

"The gatekeeper who attacked Orla came back and shot at us when we were talking to the gatekeeper at Gate 131. Then he shot him dead and disappeared into a dimensional hole."

The alien-like council member raised his voice, "How do you know the attacker was a gatekeeper?"

"He declared himself as a gatekeeper," Lorcan affirmed.

"Gatekeepers kill one another inside the Daimon Gate?" the man with the New York accent asked, shocked.

"We will make sure this is an isolated case," the Host spoke quietly.

The alien-like member shifted. "That's not why we are here. There were some discrepancies in the between the amount of information you provided us when you joined and the information we received just now. When did you declare Orla as a trained sorceress?"

Lorcan shoved his hands into his pant pockets and shrugged. "As far as I remember, we declared it right at the beginning—but not before I took the test because at that point I wasn't sure whether I had passed." A slight smile came across the Host's face. Lorcan continued, "I was always up front about Orla's talents."

"So you're saying that Orla's skills and talents in using magic were what got you both recruited?"

"Absolutely."

"All information was declared to the recruiter before you joined? Can you confirm that again?"

"Affirmative," Lorcan said, his hands clammy inside his pockets. But he trusted his poker face.

The Host showed signs of relief. The man with the alien face seemed happy with Lorcan's responses. The council member with the New York accent leaned back in his chair, contemplating, and asked, "What proof do we have of this?"

"What would you like to see?" Orla asked.

"Well, if you were recruited because of your talents, and you have had more than a month inside the Daimon Gate to learn the system and prepare, when can we expect you deliver the key to us?"

"As soon as you allow us to leave, we can get ready, investigate and dredge up a bit more information, and then we'll be on our way. As for when we can deliver the key, it depends on our progress at the site," Lorcan responded.

"Where's the site?" the alien-like man asked.

"Japan."

The council nodded in satisfaction. They had obviously never been to the place, Orla thought, as Japan was quite an enormous site to search for a little key.

The New Yorker smiled. "You know that the Host guarantees your information with his credibility, so use his trust wisely."

"Understood," Lorcan said solemnly.

Before he left with the holocast of other council members, the Host nodded slightly and smiled at Lorcan and Orla.

Once all the visitors had gone, tears poured down Orla's face. "You don't have a clue where the key is, do you, except that it might be somewhere in Japan?"

Lorcan shook his head. He pulled Orla into his arms and held her tight. "I'll figure it out," he whispered. "It's not just us now, it's the Host's credibility on the line. I don't want to think about the consequences if they find out we bluffed—and the Host endorsed it."

CHAPTER 8

Orla walked into the control room and found Lorcan still hunched over the computer. He had worked for the equivalent of thirty hours straight. They didn't use the same time reference here, so Orla had to use the computer translator for even the simplest of tasks, such as checking how long it had been since Lorcan had set foot outside that control room.

His fingers worked tirelessly on the keyboard as Orla opened the door to his office. He was so caught up in what he was doing that he didn't hear her approach and ask, "Find anything yet?"

He was startled, but he didn't let on. It was bad that he'd already lost his attention to details around him in this dimension. He'd need all of his old skills back for this assignment, and if he was this rusty, it wasn't a good sign. "I think so. I'm checking a few more things just to be sure, but I'm pretty sure I know where we'll be heading to. Are you ready?"

Orla nodded. She was back in the business mode she'd reserved for her jobs when they lived on Earth.

"The bad news is that we'll be going back to Earth. The good news is that I've found a link between the key of Psuche and a secret Japanese society called the Ryojin. We'll be heading to the Kaihanshin Prefecture. A combination of factual data, historical events, and suggestions from my underground sources led me to this conclusion, so it's not just a wild guess."

"Underground sources!" She winked at him.

He winked back, erased all of his research, and closed his computer. "We have a little time before we leave . . . how about a celebratory romp in the sack?" Orla laughed as he picked her up and carried her to their bedroom.

"Aren't you only supposed to carry me across the threshold if we get married?"

"Marry me then. Otherwise I'll be breaking the rules, and that wouldn't be good, now would it?" They both fell silent as Lorcan's innocent line reminded them that they had indeed broken the rules of this place, and death lingered at their door.

"Let's just forget about all of that right now, okay? I don't want to think about serious things right now." She rubbed her thumbs at the shadows that darted in and out of his striking blue eyes. Then she pulled his head down and kissed him, long and hard. He reciprocated her newfound level of energy and lay her on the bed, taking his shirt off before he climbed on top of her . . .

***

The trip to Japan was a nonevent. Unlike on Earth, where they had to be physically in transit, travel the distance, and face all the troubles associated with international travel, now they had only to open the portal, and in the blink of an eye, they had reached their destination.

"Welcome to Japan. We're in the second largest city in the country, next to Tokyo of course." Lorcan smiled. Orla's eyes were wide, and her mouth hung open. This was the most beautiful place she'd ever seen. It was a mix between old-world Japan and the modernization of the 21st century. She felt like this would be a wonderful place to live out the rest of her days with Lorcan if the mission should fail. She was getting ready to tell Lorcan that, but he was too busy staring at the ground. She nudged him gently, but he still didn't break his focus. She cleared her throat to no avail. She nudged him again, a little harder, trying to get his attention. He nearly stumbled and finally looked up at her. "What?"

"I wanted you to take in the beauty of this city, but all you're doing is staring at the dirt. What gives?"

He stared at her blankly for a minute, then laughed. "I'm sorry. I was trying to find someone to help us. The contact you gave me doesn't seem to be here."

"Contact?"

"Well, you told me some messenger called Kitsune would guide us. I sent a message and got a response that the messenger would be here. But I don't see anyone."

Orla laughed at Lorcan's confusion.

"Do you plan to tell me what's going on, or am I just going to learn everything as we go?" There was a definite note of irritability in his voice, and Orla knew that it was in her best interest to explain.

"A kitsune is a sort of intermediary between the world we live in and the Japanese otherworld. They're the gatekeepers that protect us from the dragons and demons that try to break through into our world. They're also damn good at finding people," Orla said solemnly, trying to keep a straight face.

"Oh, so it's not a guide-bug."

She lifted an eyebrow. "A guide-bug?"

"Like a GPS, a very advanced one."

"Oh no." Orla laughed again. "It's a magical animal. You'll know it when you see it."

"Right. But now, because we don't see it, we might have to use my robot. We need to find a woman named Chiyo Maki. She's the last surviving member of the Maki family, and they're the head family in the Ryojin group. Chiyo is a medical doctor, and she didn't seem to have much to do with the family business. But at least, it's a lead. The Ryojin group seems to have disappeared a few decades ago, but they might still have some of the items. If we're lucky, they'll have the key."

"Okay, even if they do have it, how are we going to get it from them? It's not like we packed a substantial amount of money or anything. You should have told me that we were going antique shopping." Orla smiled and winked at Lorcan. "Unless you want me to use the skills that I made a living with on Earth." Lorcan laughed. She loved that he laughed. The shadows still hovered in his eyes, but as long as he eased up a bit, she would feel much better.

Then Orla suddenly squatted down and began talking to nothingness. Lorcan blinked. The shape of a little brown fox was slowly starting to become visible. This was very interesting to him. The little thing twitched its tail and then darted off down the street a few feet, turning around to see if they were coming. "That's our guide. Let's go." Orla smiled brightly.

"It won't bite. But if it does, I'll protect you."

Lorcan shook his head. "Are you sure? I don't mind furry animals. But I'd prefer to use my technology."

She pecked Lorcan on the cheek and turned on her heel to follow the magical animal.

He shook his head again, but then followed her. "This is a mistake," he muttered.

CHAPTER 9

Two hours later, Lorcan and Orla were shuffling along on very tired feet when the little fox jumped up on a stoop and began to clean its paw. Orla thanked it, and Lorcan watched in fascination as the little fox became invisible. The only thing he could see was a distortion of the objects behind it. Then it moved, and it was gone. They were standing in front of an old Japanese house, tiered with many roofs. Lorcan pushed the doorbell, and a few minutes later, a young woman in her late twenties with long, straight black hair and deep, soulful brown eyes answered.

"Hello? May I help you?"

Lorcan donned his most charming smile. "Yes, we're looking for Doctor Chiyo Maki." He didn't want to divulge information to the wrong person, so he didn't say anything else.

"That's me. What is this about?" Her English carried a strong accent, but both Lorcan and Orla could understand her.

"We're looking to buy a unique piece from an antique collection your family owned long ago. May we come in?" The woman eyed them for a few minutes longer, then stood back so they could enter. Apparently she didn't want to discuss the delicate nature of the Royjin business in the open. She shut the door behind them and ushered them into the kitchen. The decorations were classic Japanese, but the furniture was modern. The three sat down at the kitchen table.

Something was wrong, Orla thought. It wasn't the house, or the air, but maybe the woman. *What are you up to, stranger?* Orla thought. What bothered her was the typical Japanese-style decoration in the house. Minimalist. Everything was squeaky clean. The floor looked as if you could eat from it. The conservative look on the woman's face and the tasteful decoration in the house didn't gel with the fact that the woman would invite strangers inside so easily.

"You have come to talk to me about the Royjin pieces," the woman said. It was a statement, not a question. Lorcan opened his mouth to answer, but she was already on her cell phone, speaking rapidly in Japanese. She snapped her phone shut with a little more emphasis than was necessary. "The business died with my grandfather in the Kobe earthquake of 1995. I have no involvement with it."

"Were the antiques sold to another family?" Lorcan asked.

Chiyo narrowed her eyes. "Yes."

Chiyo was lying, and Orla knew it. Lorcan didn't need Orla's psychic abilities to tell that Chiyo had lied. He glanced at Orla, and then turned back to Chiyo. "We don't mean any harm."

"Oh, I am sure you don't." The woman smiled again. "But I don't have what you need. Would you like some tea?"

"Can you tell us to which family the antiques were sold?" Lorcan asked.

"As I said, I'm not involved with the family's business. So I don't know. I'm sorry I can't help you."

"If you don't have the antiques, and you don't know where they are, then there is no point for us to bother you further," Lorcan commented.

"All right then. I'll see you to the door."

At the door, Lorcan turned around. "Do you know where we can find the family business records? Although you're not involved with the business, you would know some basic facts and some contacts such as accountants or lawyers, right?"

The woman shook her head.

"You don't know? Or you don't want to tell us?" Orla asked.

From the corner of his eye, Lorcan saw a police uniform. "Orla," he called out, gesturing in the direction of the police. Orla saw looked again at Chiyo. The woman shoved Orla and Lorcan outside the door.

"Now ask these questions to the police, you Yakuz spies!" Chiyo slammed the door closed. Orla and Lorcan glanced at the corner street. If they hurried, they could get out of here before the police arrived. They ran. They had just managed to make it a block over when they heard the sirens.

"Crazy bitch! I say we go back there and beat it out of her!" Orla was angry, and Lorcan could understand why, but he had to calm her down before she got them in trouble.

"It's okay. We'll just find another way to get the answers we need."

She cut him off with a groan. "And where exactly are we going to find these answers? Because it looks like Doctor Barbie in there doesn't want to help." Lorcan refrained from laughing at her joke because it would only encourage her.

"I have my portable laptop in the suitcase, and I can look up a few things before continue." He dug around in his suitcase for a little while, then pulled out his laptop. They were near a café, so the Wi-Fi reached their position. He typed quickly, and Orla felt a sense of pride at how good he was at his job. She stood there silently, keeping an eye out for the police while he did his search. When he snapped his laptop shut with a grin, she knew he had something.

"All right, there's a temple not too far from here, and it looks like Chiyo's grandfather's remains are there. It was a big to-do back then when they started to bury the Earthquake victims, so it wasn't too hard for me to find. Let's go."

"Not too far?"

Lorcan smiled. "About twenty minutes, darling. I can piggyback you, if that's what you'd prefer."

Orla groaned at the fact that they would be walking some more, but there was nothing to be done about it.

CHAPTER 10

Twenty minutes or so later, they'd found the temple. From the outside, there was nothing special about it. It was quiet and peaceful. The curvy roofs decorated with beautiful oriental symbols and painted with red and gold were mesmerizing. The landscape and the garden were designed and maintained meticulously with love and passion. Orla admired the temple so much that she totally forgot the gigantic problem now in front of her—the temple equals dead people, and Lorcan suffered from severe necrophobia, a fear of dead things. He had said nothing yet, but he paused on the path and looked at the temple as if it would eat him alive.

She turned and approached Lorcan, reaching out to touch his shoulders and give him comfort and assurance, but he raised his arms to stop her. "I'll be okay."

"You don't look okay." Sweat trickled down his forehead. Orla knew his hands were clammy and his heart was racing. "Are you sure?" she asked.

Lorcan nodded again. He swallowed hard, looking up at the roofs of the temples, seeing the statues of the deities guarding the gates between Heaven and Hell looking down at him. He shook his head, staring down at the ground for a short moment, and then made his way into the temple.

Inside the temple, rows and rows of remains sat in jars, marked by shiny golden plaques. Orla rolled her eyes. All the words were in Japanese. Normally, Lorcan would have automatically whisked out his device for a translation, but given his current mental status, she thought it best to remind him.

"Lorcan."

"Huh?"

"All the words are in Japanese."

"Right." No reaction from Lorcan as his eyes glazed over the rows and rows of jars containing the ashes of dead people.

"Lorcan."

"Huh?"

"All right, honey, I'll need you to get your device out and read the Japanese for me."

"Oh, that's right." He fumbled with his bag and pulled out his laptop. He used a small device to scan the text. They walked past all the plaques, and the Japanese words appeared on the screen of Lorcan's device in familiar English letters. Once they had the translation under control, it wasn't hard to find the remains of Chiyo's grandfather. The names of the individuals were written on plaques, and Orla busied herself scouting out the names.

Orla approached the jar of Chiyo's grandfather's remains to see if she could glean any information. But before she could move closer, a sea of red hair flowed in front of her. A woman slid in, standing between Orla and the ashes. The woman turned around. Her flaming red hair framed an attractive, fox-like face, long and cut with sharp angles. Orla silently admired the beauty of the woman. The woman arched an eyebrow and didn't seem to want to move.

"Excuse me, I need to see this, please." It was hard for Orla to be polite when she was still felt outrage at Chiyo's treatment of them, but she did her best. The woman gave her a look she couldn't read, but she didn't move. Orla's blood was starting to boil. "Look, I'm on a mission here, lady, and you're in my way. So step back for a minute." The woman didn't say anything to her, nor did she step away. Orla grabbed her shoulder to push her back a little, but the woman's hands came up lightning fast, breaking her grip before she'd been moved an inch. Orla's temper got the better of her, and she reached out to slap the woman. The woman grabbed Orla's hand before it hit her. She looked stunned at what Orla had just done. She rocked back on her feet and struck a fighting position. Orla grinned at her and took her own fighting stance— she was in the mood for a good fight.

"No, no, women, we're in a temple, for God's sake." Lorcan charged over to pull Orla aside. At the same time, Fox Face flew through the air and landed a kick which had been intended for Orla, but hit Lorcan's back instead. He stumbled and turned around. "Look, I don't fight women, okay. But if you keep attacking my wife, I'll make an exception."

"We're not married yet, you can't call me your wife, and I don't need you to protect me." Orla snarled and leaped at Fox Face. Fox Face turned quickly and gave Orla a roundhouse kick, connecting with Orla's middle and sending her reeling backwards, rolling outside of the temple.

Orla stood up, wheezing. Lorcan went after her. Once outdoors, he was back to his alert self. Fox Face was approaching Orla, a knowing smile on her face. Orla wanted to wipe that smile off with her foot. She lunged at the woman, tackling her around the waist and throwing her to the ground. Either Fox Face hadn't been trained in grappling, or she was just stunned to find herself on the floor with Orla on top of her, because she let Orla get a good punch in to her face before she began to protect herself.

"I know you understood what I was saying. Want to tell me why you wouldn't move?" Orla was giving her a chance to talk, but it was really just to gloat over the bruise that was blooming ever so nicely on the woman's pale face. Fox Face didn't respond, and that angered Orla even further. But what Orla didn't see until it was arcing towards her chest was the knife that Fox Face had pulled out of nowhere. Orla let out a squeal and threw her arm down at an angle, forcing the blade and its wielding arm go in an entirely different direction. The woman dropped the knife, and it skittered across the worn cobblestones until it came to rest at Lorcan's feet. He picked it up and pocketed it quickly before anyone could see what had happened.

"No, Orla, don't fight. We've got things to do." Lorcan tried to hold her back, but then the woman tried to run at Orla. "Hey lady, calm down. Let's talk." Lorcan stood in the way to stop her from jumping on Orla. She gave him a hard kick, pushing him to the ground. Lorcan stood. "That's enough! This is stupid." He grabbed the woman from behind while she scuffled with Orla and dragged her away. The woman wriggled but couldn't release herself from Lorcan's grip. She snarled and shouted for release in Japanese. Lorcan didn't need the device to translate—he knew what she was cursing about. He refused to let go, dragging her as far away from Orla as possible. As Lorcan's right arm wrapped around the woman's neck from behind, she tilted her head and bit at his right wrist. As soon as her teeth sank into his flesh, he loosed his grip and staggered back. He leaned against a tree, holding on to it to keep his balance. He felt as if the ground under his feet was moving.

The woman stumbled backward. She kept her stance, wiped her mouth, and locked her gaze on Lorcan. Then her skin began to glow all over in a warm shade of light, and seconds later, a red fox sat in front of an astonished Lorcan and Orla. Before Orla could pulled her jaw closed, the fox darted over and bit Orla, then scampered away. It was making its way to the temple exit when Orla pulled her own knife out of her boot and threw it at the fox. The fox stopped and transformed back into the red-haired woman, throwing a blaze of flame in Orla's direction. Unfortunately, the blast of flame rerouted the knife Orla had thrown, and it ended up striking Lorcan instead.

He caught the impact of the knife and the fire at the same time.

CHAPTER 11

The fox woman ran away, and Orla threw herself to the ground next to Lorcan. She didn't have to be a doctor to know that he was injured very badly . . . again. "Hey. Hang in there for me, okay? I'm going to take you somewhere where they can help you. Just hang in there for me."

Lorcan opened his mouth to speak, but he couldn't force any sound past his lips. He hated to see the tears welling in Orla's eyes. He tried, but he wasn't able to move. Yet his mind was crystal clear. There was a surge of something strange running through his body, and he didn't care for it. It was burning hot. It wasn't the wounds that held him down. It was something else, something new. He forced his eyes open.

Orla caressed his face. "Okay Lorcan, you have to try for me. I can't carry you. Come on, baby, sit up for me." Lorcan summoned as much energy as he could, and with her help, he sat up. It felt like being inside a front-loading washing machine.

They stood up, and Orla wrapped his arm around her shoulders. Step by step, the made it along the narrow road back to the village. Chiyo was a medical doctor. Orla had no idea where else to go. She didn't know where a medical center or hospital might be. She didn't speak Japanese and couldn't understand the street signs and storefronts. There wasn't any time for her to regret that she could have been a bit more cultural.

She backtracked as far as she needed to get to Chiyo's house, and she only got lost once. Lorcan stumbled to the ground a couple of times, but he kept up. At the house, she rang the doorbell and waited. Chiyo came to the door.

"You again! I will not have spies in my house! I'm calling the police."

Orla leaned Lorcan up against the side of the house and grabbed the woman by the throat. "Listen here. He's very badly hurt, and you're a doctor. We're not spies or lunatics. I just want you to help him. I'm pretty sure your Hippocratic Oath says that you can do no harm. If you send us back out into the streets, he's going to die, and I'm pretty sure that death counts as harm, so how about you let us in and tend to him?" Before Chiyo could answer, Lorcan's eyes rolled back, and he fell face down onto the ground, half in and half out of the house.

The woman reached up and gently removed Orla's fingers from her throat. "If he stays like that, I can't close the door, either with you in or outside of my house. Bring him in. I'll see what I can do." The two women struggled with Lorcan's dead weight, but they were able to lay him on the living room floor, tucked among the cushions. Chiyo disappeared into the next room and then came bustling in with a black leather doctor's bag. She pointed to the corridor. "The guest room is upstairs on the left."

"What?"

"Close the door on your way out."

"Huh?"

"You want me to treat him or not?"

"Yes, of course. Please. But can I stay?"

Chiyo glared at Orla.

"I guess not," Orla muttered and turned on her heel. She didn't go upstairs to the guest room but waited outside. It seemed like decades. Orla sat on the floor, leaning against the wall, and fell asleep. When she woke and tried to get back into the living room, the door was locked. "Doctor my ass," Orla muttered and sat back down on the floor.

CHAPTER 12

Orla wasn't at all happy with being locked out, but she knew she couldn't be pushy right now because Lorcan's life hung in Chiyo's hands. She waited for what seemed like hours, pacing back and forth in the hallway, thinking that she might actually see the carpet start to fray under her feet. When the door finally opened, Orla ran to it and tried to push through, but Chiyo stood in her way.

"He's asleep right now. You can't go in there. He's lucky to be alive with those injuries." Her voice was hard, and she cast a condescending look at Orla.

"Watch your tone, doc. I would've taken the knife for him if I could have, regardless of whether he was happy about it or not." She got the words out through teeth gritted in anger.

Chiyo just shrugged and walked away.

"Listen here. If it weren't for the fact that you threw us out of your house instead of offering to help us, we wouldn't have had to go there to search for your grandfather's remains." That stopped Chiyo short. She turned around, anger flashing from her eyes, and her cheeks growing red.

"How dare you defile my grandfather's memory by looking for him like common grave robbers! I'm sure I'm not the only one who's ever told you no. I think you need to start taking rejection a little better."

Orla was barely controlling herself, and her hands were clenched into shaking fists at her sides when she threw her next verbal barb. "Grave robbers? Look who's talking. This might be beyond your understanding, but in the place we call home, someone from here—very possibly a member of your extended family—robbed a man of a key and buried him in a wall, leaving him to rot. We're simply try to retrieve the key and return it. So don't you dare stick that robber label on us."

"Robbery and murder? What exactly are you accusing my family of?" Chiyo snarled.

"Look at who is not taking criticism well *now*."

"You're only guests in my house. Remember that I can kick you out again at any time."

***

Lorcan woke in the living room. Opening his eyes and at the blurry edges of his vision, he saw elegant wallpaper and tastefully arranged furniture. He felt his body comfortably tucked under a thick blanket. He could hear the argument between Orla and Chiyo echoing in from the corridor. He tried to shift, but his limbs seemed to weigh a ton. He closed his eyes, concentrated, and tried to take mental inventory. He had been dragging a woman away from Orla when the woman bit him and then turned into a fox. He remembered it now. All of it. The sensation of her teeth sinking into his flesh. It hadn't hurt, but he remembered the inexplicable feeling of something flooding into him. It was like her bite had flipped a switch and opened a floodgate, except what poured into him wasn't water but something else. Exactly what, he wasn't sure.

He opened his eyes again and found his vision and strength had improved significantly. He shifted, freed his hands, and felt the blanket rub against his skin. He lifted it, looking underneath, and as he predicted, he was half naked. The wound on his abdomen had been dressed carefully. Lorcan shifted and sat up. For a split second, he saw the skin on his arm glow an electric blue. He shook his head and looked again—his skin had gone back to normal.

"What the fuck!" Lorcan mumbled to himself and sat up, leaning against a low coffee table nearby. It was clear to him that the two women hadn't been able to move his dead weight without doing more damage to him, so they had treated him right on the floor in the middle of the living room. He felt as if energy was returning to him in strong waves—it was the same healing feeling he'd had when Orla used the dark magic to heal him in London. It was also the very reason they'd had to take refuge in the Daimon Gate. "Oh, why did you do that again, Orla?" he mumbled to himself. He grabbed his shirt, which was folded neatly on the coffee table nearby, and put it on.

He shook his head, feeling uneasy. Something strange was growing inside him.

CHAPTER 13

Lorcan found Orla with her hands on her hips at the end of the corridor by the kitchen, snarling at Chiyo, who was responding in a no less aggressive manner. The scene made Lorcan want to chuckle, but he didn't think it wise to risk aggravating the situation.

"How's a man supposed to get any sleep around here with you women practicing your Christmas carols," Lorcan said from the doorway. Orla turned around and blushed a little as she came over to his side, hugging him gently.

"You shouldn't be up. You were hurt very badly, and you can't heal if you don't rest." There was a sternness to Chiyo's voice again, and Orla recognized that she'd turned back into a doctor.

"I think you'll find that I'm doing much better already." He winked at Orla, and she smiled.

Chiyo obviously didn't appreciate her patients talking back to her. "Go lie back down, and I'll look you over." She donned an arrogant tone and stared at Lorcan as sternly as she could. Lorcan nodded and returned to the living room. Orla trailed right behind him, being sure to sneak into the room before Chiyo this time so the other woman couldn't throw her out. Lorcan did as he was told and lay back down on the blanket. Chiyo rummaged through her doctor's bag and took out her stethoscope. She listened to his heart and lungs, claiming they were back to a normal rhythm. She lifted the bandage to have a look at the wound.

"You're doing very well," Chiyo concluded. Her tone was as smooth as still water, but her face betrayed her. Catching the look, Orla narrowed her eyes. She opened her mouth to say something, but in anticipation, Lorcan shook his head, signaling Orla not to say anything. She obliged.

Chiyo cleared her throat. "You wound has healed." Orla arched an eyebrow and said nothing as Chiyo began to remove Lorcan's bandages. His injuries looked like they'd been healing for weeks instead of barely an hour. "How did you do this? If you could do this by yourself, then why did you come to me for help? You're recovering faster than I've ever seen anyone recover. It's a medical mystery. One that I would like to study."

"He's not a lab rat in a drug trial. You're not going to study him." Orla spat her words at the doctor. "And if he's healed, may we have a moment in private?" Orla was surprised by the politeness of her voice.

Lorcan smiled. "I need to talk to her, doc. Would you mind stepping out for a few minutes?"

Chiyo glared at both of them, but kept her voice toned down. "You still need rest. The guest room upstairs on the left is yours. You'll have your privacy there. I'm not leaving my own living room."

Lorcan nodded. "Understood. I appreciate that." He stood and went upstairs with Orla.

***

Inside the guest room, Orla flipped Lorcan's shirt up and stared at the healing wound. "How did you manage to heal so quickly? The first time it was because I helped you, but this time, I know it wasn't me." Orla kept her voice low because she had the sneaking suspicion that Chiyo was listening at the door.

"I thought I was the one who'd be asking the questions. I thought you'd used the black magic again."

Orla shook her head. "I'm not stupid enough to summon my ancestors while we're in a place where we can't go anywhere without your translator and my guide fox. In that case, we shouldn't bother with the key at all because we'd soon be dead."

"The key is no longer just *our* problem, Orla. The Host is now involved in all this."

"I know, I know."

"So you really didn't use any magic on me this time?"

Orla stared at Lorcan. "Hey, you're healed, but not a hundred percent yet. I can hurt you. You don't want to upset me."

Lorcan raised his arms, seeking peace and a truce. Orla smiled, tiptoed, and kissed him. She pulled him into her arms and embraced him, her body shuddering with emotions. "Oh God, you went down like a stone." He held on to her and kissed her forehead. "I know I scared you. I'm sorry."

"It's not your fault. The bitch bit you."

Lorcan nodded. "Not everyone has a chance to be bitten by a fox. I told you I'm not a fan of furry animals."

"It's not remotely funny."

Lorcan glanced at the small window which overlooked the roof of the ground level of the house. He felt something crawling underneath his skin. He shook his head and frowned.

"What are you not telling me?" Orla asked.

"What?"

"You heard me. You have that I'm-not-telling-her-just-yet face."

"I don't even know what that means."

She jabbed her finger at his chest. "You know what I mean. You're a smart-ass. You always know." She pushed him so that he was off-balance and fell down to the futon.

"Now that we have a room to ourselves, what do you say we really celebrate my ability to heal so quickly?" He wiggled his eyebrows at her, and Orla felt herself laugh for the first time in what seemed like weeks. She wriggled against him, and he groaned into her ear. "You know, if you don't stop that, I'm not going to be accountable for my actions, missy."

Orla didn't say a word, just wriggled against him again.

CHAPTER 14

A pale fox-like face stared back at her from the mirror. It had been a long time since she had spared a moment for such vanity. People told her she was beautiful, but what was the use of her beauty? she wondered. She was raised to be the female alpha of her werefox clan, a rare group with an important and sacred mission that had started before her time, but now she just wanted to be an ordinary woman, entitled to live a life with the freedom to love and have a family.

She had bitten a man today. The tradition of the werefoxes was that biting was a mating ritual. Unless forced or acting in self-defense, biting marked a mate for life. When a fox chose a mating partner, it all started with an intentional bite. It was like human consensual sex. She smiled at the thought. She spent way too much time with humans.

The rules didn't apply in her case because she had bitten in self-defense, and he was human. She could bite and kill any other creatures except foxes. She touched her lips. The tingling sensation of his blood on her lips and in her mouth still remained. *What is this man?* she thought. She had bitten humans before, but they had tasted nothing like this. His blood had actually forced her to shift into her fox form right in the middle of a fight.

***

Lorcan stared up to the ceiling, contemplating the next move for both of them. He sat up abruptly and jumped out of the futon. He heard Orla giggle. Lorcan looked down and darted back to the futon to grab his pants and put them on. He pulled out his laptop, started it, and sat on the floor to work.

"What do you have in mind?" Orla asked.

Lorcan didn't hear her. He typed quickly, mumbled, cursed to himself, then typed again. Orla rolled deeper into the blanket. When Lorcan was engaged in his tech world, the smartest thing for her to do was to treat herself to a nap.

"Whoa, whoa! No! Fuck!" Lorcan's curses drew Orla out of her daydream.

"What's up, Lorcan?"

"Lost the signals. Goddamn it."

Orla narrowed her eyes. "You're not hooking up to your system in the Daimon Gate, are you?"

He nodded. "Just a thought coming across my mind. The gatekeeper who attacked you, he wanted to bring Ciaran down. Exposing a computer manipulation is pretty low. But what if that's all he's got? All he was thinking about? Think about that incident again, Orla. Apart from you and me, who else knows about this within the Daimon Gate? No one except Prince Brandon, right?"

Orla sat up. "But Ciaran risked his life to change the data in the system to save Brandon. Why would Brandon want to harm Ciaran?"

"Well, that's what I was checking into before I lost the signals. Ciaran mentioned that the princess had cheated the system—that's why both the prince and the princess were facing the death penalty. Ciaran also said he owed the prince a favor, so he manipulated the system to reduce the death sentence to a demotion."

"Shouldn't Brandon be grateful for that?"

"Well, I would, if it were me, Orla. But a guy like Brandon, a guy who would attack a woman and kill an unarmed helpless man, wouldn't behave in the same way as a rational person would. What if he considered the demotion to be worse than death? Maybe he would rather die than losing his privilege. In that case, by saving them, Ciaran may have actually taken away the prince's right to die in privilege."

"Who would have thought about that?"

"It's not rational. Definitely not normal. But it can't be as rare as being bitten by a fox!" Lorcan smiled.

"You bet. So you think the gatekeeper who attacked me is Prince Brandon?"

Lorcan nodded. "Pretty sure of it now. The data suggested he was demoted from gatekeeper of the Red Castle to a minor gatekeeper of a creek. It was like a sympathy demotion, a token position. That would have been an insult to him. And also, the data suggests that he had dismissed himself from his position yesterday and vanished."

"Vanished?"

"Outside the Daimon Gate. My prediction is that after attacking us at Gate 131 and killing the defenseless gatekeeper there, he knew he would be facing severe punishment, so he fled."

"Sadistic son of a bitch will seek revenge on us. If he returned Ciaran's favor by vengeance, what would he make of us reporting him to the Host and aggravating his already bad situation?"

Lorcan smiled. "He'll turn into a little ghost and haunt us for the rest of our lives."

Orla sat up, pressing her forehead head to her knees. "I can deal with ghosts."

Lorcan crawled over and hugged her. "You're not doing anything by yourself. We'll do it together. Personally, I prefer animals to ghosts," Lorcan whispered.

She looked up at him, "You're thinking of the werefox?"

Lorcan rubbed his nose into Orla's hair and muffled, "Now *that* animal is definitely weird and mysterious. I'm not sure of my preference anymore. Can I lie down for another minute?"

"Sure you can."

CHAPTER 15

Later that night, Orla was snuggling next to Lorcan, trying to sleep, when she sat bolt upright. She thought she'd heard something downstairs. She tried to look into the darkness around her with her dulled vision, but she could see only shadows and vague shapes. She was ready to lie down again, chalking it up to a figment of her imagination, but then she heard it again. It was a faint tapping sound, almost like in the movies where archaeologists tap away at artifacts with tiny hammers and chisels. She reached her hand out to

Lorcan, gently shaking his shoulder. He mumbled in his sleep and rolled away from her.

Sitting in the dark, listening to the noises becoming steadily louder, a sheen of sweat beaded on her forehead. She began searching the dark room for something close at hand she might be able to use as a weapon. If she got up, whoever was breaking in downstairs would hear her and probably run away before they had a chance to question him.

"Lorcan! Wake up! Someone's breaking in downstairs." Her voice quavered a little as she whispered, and she was mildly embarrassed by it. She was not usually easily scared, unless it came to Lorcan getting hurt. She felt like one of those hysterical women in horror movies who always ended up dead because they were stupid. She shook him again, and this time he woke up. He opened his mouth to ask her what was going on, but then he heard it, too. He sat up like Orla, looking around as she had for a weapon.

"Do you really think we'll need weapons? I think the two of us can handle him together. Come on. It's the least we can do for our host." The sarcasm dripping from Orla's voice almost made Lorcan laugh, but he held back.

The two of them slid out of the room, inching along the corridor by trying to step only on areas of the floor that wouldn't creak. They managed to get downstairs, although to Orla it felt like it took an hour. As they crept into the kitchen, they could see the soft moonlight shining down on a figure climbing in through the little window over the sink. They stood in the shadows, one on either side of the doorway, waiting for him to come close enough for the first blow. Orla had to control herself because the intruder was really bungling the situation. He'd gotten part of his shoe stuck in the garbage disposal, and she had to ignore the urge to turn it on. Lorcan must have been fighting an urge to laugh as well because she saw his hand go to his mouth.

The man finally got himself situated, presumably cursing in Japanese. He wore a nice suit, and she thought that a little odd for a late night intrusion. He straightened his suit, then reached behind him, through the window, to pick up a small bouquet of roses. Okay, this had now become the strangest break-in that Orla had ever witnessed. And she'd been a part of quite a few. She stepped forward and dealt the man a quick blow to the nose, sending him reeling back. He threw his arms into the sink to steady himself. The roses went flying, and Lorcan ran to catch them. The man was blabbering in Japanese, which neither Orla nor Lorcan could understand, but at one point he raised his voice and yelled Chiyo's name. Not two seconds later, a loud clattering came down the stairs, and Chiyo raced into the kitchen, turning on the lights. She was dressed to the nines, ready for a night out on the town. She'd managed to get a later shift at the hospital, and she'd been waiting for her date.

"Stop! What are you doing?" Chiyo assessed the situation quickly, then darted between Orla and the man, holding her hands out to halt the next punch. "Leave him alone!"

"I don't know if you noticed, but this piece of trash here just broke in through your window. Do you want to be kidnapped and murdered in the middle of the night? It looks like you dressed the part." Orla's drawl made Chiyo's cheeks turn red, and she didn't look happy at all.

"Why don't you sit down, and we'll explain." Chiyo had one hand up to her head like she was suffering from a very annoying headache. The man in the suit sat down at the kitchen table, put his hands in front of him, and waited quietly. Chiyo sat down, too, motioning for Orla and Lorcan to follow suit. They did so, but both of them now had suspicion in their eyes. "I'll start from the beginning. This man is Goro Kagome. He used to belong to the group Yakuz."

Lorcan interrupted. "You mean he's one of those spies that you accused *us* of being? You threw us out without even listening!" Lorcan was beginning to let anger win out over curiosity, and that usually wasn't a good sign.

"He's not Yakuz anymore. He left them. It was difficult because he belonged to the worst branch of them, but he did it. We've been together for a while now, and the only way that we can see each other is in secret. I should have warned you that I had guests, Goro. I'm sorry." Chiyo turned to look at the pair across the table from her. "And I'm sorry that I didn't warn you that he was coming tonight. It would have saved us all a lot of trouble."

Lorcan threw the roses at her. "Then I guess these are for you."

CHAPTER 16

Lorcan didn't know how late it was or what kind of nightlife was still going on at this hour, but he did know that he was tired after three rounds of lovemaking, and right now he wanted nothing more than to fall asleep with Orla in his arms. Orla had hoped for a restful and uneventful rest of the evening, but alas, there was no rest for the wicked. She yawned as she rose from the table, and it told Lorcan that she was thinking along the same lines as he was. He put his arm around her, and the two of them headed back up to bed.

The rays of the rising sun were just beginning to peek through the lace of the curtains when Orla sat up again. There was a distinct clicking noise coming from downstairs that sounded like the heels of a man's very expensive pair of shoes. She rolled over and closed her eyes again. There was no way she was going to lose any more sleep over Chiyo's idiot boyfriend. But it took her only a few minutes to remember that she'd seen Goro's shoes, and they were not the kind that had heels that clicked. Eyes wide, she sat up again and listened. Her movement caused Lorcan to sit up, too, and she held a finger to her mouth to indicate that he should be quiet. He took her hand and listened with her.

"I don't think that's Goro. He has different shoes."

Lorcan raised an eyebrow. "We were fighting someone we thought to be a dangerous intruder, and you paid attention to his *shoes?*"

Orla shrugged. "It was after we figured out he was Chiyo's boyfriend. I thought his shoes would look good on you."

"No, thank you. I can choose my own outfits."

"Should we bother to look downstairs? Or will it only be a waste of time?"

Lorcan was silent for a minute, then shrugged. "I think we should at least take a look at what's going on. If there's a plausible reason for another visitor, then so be it. If not, well, we can let the poor bastard have it."

Orla grinned in the semi-darkness. Once again, the two of them crept out of bed and slid down the stairs in near perfect silence. When they came to the hallway, they saw a massive figure looming in the doorway. It was clear to the both of them that this was definitely not Goro. Orla blinked, shook her head, blinked again, and stared. Lorcan's eyes widened.

The man had no eyes. He held his hands out in front of him, and in the middle of each palm was a large, monstrous-looking eye. The pupils were slitted like those of a cat, and they gave Orla the creeps. There was no way that this . . . thing was supposed to be in Chiyo's house, so she did the one thing that she could think of. Orla curved her fists and sent jets of flame at him, setting him on fire. He stumbled around a little bit, setting a few things around him on fire as well, but Orla did a good job of controlling the flames.

A shadowy figure danced in through the open door, darting in and out of the flames with such speed that Orla and Lorcan knew it wasn't human. When the figure paused in front of them, they recognized the fox from the temple. The fox ran up the stairs like she owned the place.

"You take Palm-Eyes, and I'll take care of the animal," Orla said, and before Lorcan could speak, she ran after the fox. She crested the stairs just in time to see the little red tail disappear into Chiyo's room. Orla swore. Now she'd have to protect that hoity-toity bitch, and she wasn't thrilled about that at all. When she threw the door open, however, the room was empty except for the foxy woman digging through Chiyo's belongings. Orla planted herself in the doorway and cleared her throat.

The fox-faced woman stood up. As she had shifted from her fox form back into human form, she was wearing nothing but a tiny red bikini. Orla blinked. The suit must be designed from a special material designed to protect the woman when she morphed into different forms. On top of an exquisite face, Orla had to admit that the woman had a flawless body. It must come with the fox genes, Orla mused.

"What are you doing here? I didn't like you at the temple, and I don't like you now. What are you looking for?" She hoped that her sheer bluntness would startle an answer out of the woman, but she was wrong. The woman turned back into the little fox and darted out of the room between Orla's legs, scampering down the stairs. She screamed out for Lorcan to grab her at the bottom, but she didn't know if he could hear her over the crackling of the flames.

By the time Orla made it to the foot of the stairs, the foxy woman was back, standing over the body of the man with eyes on his hands. She tilted her head back and opened her mouth in a mournful sound that Orla and Lorcan had never heard before. The woman stared them down, and then she began to scream for Chiyo. Chiyo, of course, didn't answer because she still hadn't come home yet from her date.

"Look, I don't know who or what you are, but listen to me and stop that wailing for a minute!" Orla's angry voice pierced through the woman's screams like a hot knife through butter. In utter shock, she stopped her strange noise and looked at Orla. "Thank you. Chiyo isn't here right now, but I want you to know that she's protected. So back off and leave her alone."

The woman shook her head. "If Chiyo is with that boyfriend of hers, then she's going to be in trouble." The woman turned and tried to leave, but Orla and Lorcan were hot on her trail. Waving her hand in an intricate pattern, Orla removed the flame from the building and swung the door closed.

She and Lorcan were now in pursuit of the little fox, but it was very difficult to see her in the early morning light. Neither of them were exactly dressed for a manhunt, but they would have to tough it out. They needed to find out who and what this fox was, and why she was after Chiyo.

CHAPTER 17

Orla and Lorcan followed Fox Face as she darted through the city. It really was a lot easier to follow someone when there weren't hundreds of people in the way. As they trailed this mysterious creature, she led them farther and farther away from the center of the city. After a while, it looked like they were in a part of the city that was crammed full of warehouses for the various businesses in town. Fox Face hauled open a door to one of the larger warehouses.

Orla and Lorcan watched from a distance for a few minutes to see if she would come back out. When she didn't, Lorcan swore and motioned for Orla to follow him. The two of them crept in through still-cracked door, and the scene that met them was a grisly one. Chiyo was tied to a pillar in the back of the empty warehouse, her hands above her head and her feet barely touching the ground. There was a group of mooks threatening the young doctor. Tears were running down her face.

The conversation was in Japanese. Lorcan pulled out his palm device and turned it on. It captured the sound signals, and soon English text flew onto the little screen.

"I don't know what you're talking about. I've never seen a key!" Chiyo cried.

A thin man paced back and forth in front of Chiyo, a malicious smile on his face. "Maybe I can help you remember." He snapped his fingers and four mooks came from nowhere, a platform balanced on their shoulders. They set the platform down, and took the dirty blanket off of the misshapen form wriggling underneath. Orla gasped and had to put her hands over her mouth to stifle it. On the platform was Goro, Chiyo's boyfriend. His hands were tied behind his back, and he had a heavy manacle around his neck with four chains coming down to attach to four iron rings on the platform. He was kneeling, and he had what looked to be a dirty bandana in his mouth as a gag. When he saw Chiyo, he struggled, trying to break free and get to her. Orla felt tears in eyes when she saw that. She shifted and turned back, seeing Lorcan looking at her. He kissed her on the cheek.

"Now, maybe you can tell me a little more about the key of Psuche?" the man's voice slid out like poisoned silk. Chiyo yanked at her restraints, and Lorcan saw blood running down her wrists.

"I don't know anything about it! I'm just a doctor! My grandfather had the antique business, but it died with him in the earthquake! Please, let us go. I swear I don't know anything." She was crying now.

Orla wanted to jump in for a rescue. She hopped up, but Lorcan held her back. "We're seriously outnumbered," he said.

"Poor little Chiyo. It looks like things are going to get worse for you before they get better. Think hard. Is there anything that you remember? Anything at all?" the man grumbled.

Chiyo was silent for a few minutes. "All I can remember is that it was a metal key with a stone on the top of it. I don't remember what kind of stone— or even if it did anything special. I was only a child, and I had nothing to do with the antique business. That's all I know, I swear. Please, just let us go."

The man stared at Chiyo hard, like he was trying to see down into her very soul to determine whether she was telling the truth. "I believe you. I really do. The only problem is, the mooks don't." He spread his arms wide in an 'I don't know' gesture. Chiyo's eyes grew wide with fear, and he swung his head in Goro's direction.

"No, no, please don't do that!" Chiyo cried.

The man pointed at Goro. "What about you? Do you know?"

Chiyo shook her head. "No no, he doesn't know anything."

"We have no use for him then," the man concluded and signaled the mooks. One of them drew a katana from a sheath at his side, walked up soundlessly behind Goro, and slit his throat with one swipe. Chiyo screamed and fainted.

Lorcan had reached his limit. He stepped out into the open space. Orla started to follow, but she was grabbed from behind. Lorcan and Orla turned around, ready for a fight, when they saw Fox Face.

"You're going to need more than just the two of you." The fox woman's voice was low, and she was trying to speak urgently to Orla without anyone overhearing her.

Before Orla and Lorcan had a chance to respond, Fox Face stumbled backward until she was almost even with the pillar Chiyo was tied to. She didn't even know what hit her. The mooks had made them and had attacked from behind.

Fox Face stood up slowly, rubbing her rib cage, wheezing. Men poured out from nowhere, attacking them from left, right, and center. Orla was separated from Lorcan. Three dangerous-looking goons approached her. She stepped back and saw about ten of them pounding on Lorcan. She clenched her jaw. *You forced me to do this*, she thought as she curved her hands into fists and sent fire balls flying at the criminals. She soon cleared out the three who were attacking her. She turned to Lorcan and saw he had knocked down five men, bare-handed, but before she could do anything, a goon standing behind Lorcan pulled out a knife and stabbed him.

Lorcan slumped to the ground.

CHAPTER 18

Orla thought she had stopped breathing. She darted forward, and fireballs flew at the criminal like fireworks. In the haze of confusion, smoke, and the smell of burnt flesh, she didn't realize she had cleared the entire gang out with her fire and Fox Face had just knocked down the last man standing.

Orla knelt down in front of Lorcan, gently stroking his cheek. "Lorcan? Can you hear me? Talk to me, baby."

He groaned and opened his eyes. "I hate it when women are still standing, and I'm the one lying on the ground. You've got to teach me some of that magic of yours."

"Sure thing." Orla helped him sit up.

"I'll heal, as you've already seen."

"All right. But it'll still take a while. Now stand up for me." She slid her arm around his waist. "There you go." He stood up straight, stumbled a few steps, then straightened up again.

"I'm okay. Where's Chiyo? Did you get her out yet?" Orla shook her head. She slowly led Lorcan toward the other end of the warehouse where Fox Face was standing.

Lorcan tried not to lean a lot of his weight on Orla. He couldn't quite figure out how his healing ability had been triggered before. At the moment, he didn't think it was working. The wound on his back was searing, and blood was streaming out. His vision became more blurry by the second. He walked a few more steps with Orla's assistance and then started to stagger. "I . . . I don't think I can . . ." he slurred out and then dropped to the floor in a heap.

"Oh my God!" Orla cried out. She looked up and saw Fox Face approaching. She still didn't trust her, but she really didn't have a choice at the moment. They carried Lorcan to the corner where Chiyo was tied up, and leaned him against a pillar.

"He'll heal. He's like us. But all creatures have different ways of healing. He might have to shut down his system before the healing can start," Fox Face said.

"What? What do you mean by he's 'like' you?" Orla snarled.

"I thought you knew."

"Knew what?"

Fox Face shook her head. "We have other matters to see to now. I'm not yet sure about him, so it's better not to make assumptions."

"The hell I'll let you get away with this. The last time it took hours for him to recover from your knife. Now you're say he's like *you*? Like what? A werefox?"

"I said I'm not sure."

Orla grumbled some profanity and then pulled Lorcan into her, resting his head on her shoulder. She flipped the back of his shirt up and could see his wound was starting to heal. She looked up at Fox Face and saw a faint smirk flash across her face, but she let it go for now. She leaned Lorcan back again on the pillar. Then she went over to Chiyo and started to pick the lock on her manacles. Fox Face admired Orla's skills.

"Wow, you're good."

Orla looked at her, then decided to swallow her snarky response. She lay Chiyo down to the floor and came back to Lorcan. "We have to get out of here soon. I don't know when they'll be back."

"I agree. We can't stay here for long."

Orla gestured at Lorcan and Chiyo. "Can't go anywhere with these two dead-weight bodies here."

"It's dangerous here. I know a place where we can regroup. But we'll have to wait until these two can walk by themselves. At the moment, I hope the Gods here would protect us."

"Here? In this warehouse? Since when that God has changed his style of residence?" Orla asked.

A wave of sadness poured from Fox Face's eyes. "On this very ground used to be an old temple that was abandoned generations ago. The people in the city think it's haunted, so they don't come here, and they've never had the nerve to bulldoze it down." There was a wistfulness to her tone, and it softened Orla's temper just a little.

"Why do people think it's haunted?" she asked gently.

Fox Face looked down at the ground at her feet.

"This temple used to honor us Kitsune, but almost everyone has forgotten us now. There are still those select few that come here to honor us or pray to us for help, but that number dwindles more and more with each passing year."

"You were after Chiyo. Same with the mooks. You're after the key, too. Do these gangsters know you?" Orla did her best to keep her anger at bay, but some of it bled into her voice anyway. Fox Face dropped her gaze. She didn't want to answer, and Orla realized that she really didn't have any way of making her if she didn't want to. She wasn't a bully, per se, unless she had to be one to finish a job.

Lorcan began to stir. Orla went over, and seeing him open his eyes slightly and smile at her, she knew he would heal quickly from this point. She kissed his cheek. Lorcan was beginning to get that twinkle back in his eyes that said he was alert and ready for danger. His injuries seemed to be healing as quickly as they had at Chiyo's house.

Fox Face spoke up again. "I want to apologize for not introducing myself. My name is Mori. I'm a werefox, a creature of folklore. Even though we sometimes walk as humans, we never forget who and what we are. In order to keep ourselves secret from the world, we tend to go underground a lot. That was how I met the Yakuz."

Orla was very sick and tired of hearing that word and not knowing what it meant. "What exactly are these Yakuz?" If she had to fight them again, then she wanted to know what they were up against.

"They are humanoid in form, but they have certain, otherworldly features to them. The man you killed in Chiyo's apartment? He was a tenome, a Yakuz. You could ask her boyfriend for more information if the mooks hadn't killed him. There are myriad creatures and people belonging to that group—even I don't know all of their names. They are very powerful, and the Kitsune stays out of their way." She blushed at this debasement of her breed, but it was the truth, and so she had to reveal it. "The eyes in the man's palms don't see only the mundane as humans do, they see the ghosts of souls past and what they did when they were alive. He was sent to her apartment to find out what she knew about the key of Psuche. I don't know what he saw, but I know that he didn't gather any information from Chiyo, and the fact that the two of you killed him will slow down the Yakuz as well. Take pride in what you've done. Not very many otherworldly creatures could have rid themselves of him if he had come knocking, and here you are, two humans, taking out one of the Yakuz by yourselves." Mori sounded impressed, even though it was obvious that she was trying to hide that fact from them.

Orla narrowed her eyes. "But you seemed sad when the Palm-eye died."

Mori looked at Orla, "Did I?" Then she came back to her usual silent mode and ignored Orla unanswered question.

They heard a clanking sound at the far end of the warehouse.

"Oh hell, they're back already." Orla stood.

"Yep." Mori darted over, standing next to Orla. Lorcan grumbled and tried to stand up. Orla used one hand to squash him back down to the floor. From the far end of the warehouse, a group of twelve menacing men strode in.

CHAPTER 19

"How many of them can you take?" Orla asked Mori as she gestured toward the coming men. Orla looked around and grabbed a steel bar close by. Lorcan tried to stand up again. She darted over, not squashing him down this time but dragging him behind the pillar. Lorcan's eyes sparked with anger, but he couldn't resist—Orla was much stronger than he was at the moment.

Mori watched the couple with amusement and felt an unusual feeling slash at her heart. It felt like a pain, but she wasn't sure exactly what it was, so she let it go. "I can take five of them in my human form," she told Orla.

Orla glanced at her. The beautiful woman was in bare feet and wore only her swimsuit. "What about in your fox form?"

Mori grinned. "Well, as an animal, I don't count. But I can take all of them."

"Arrogant bitch. Don't be greedy," Orla snarled.

"I'll leave you a couple then." Mori grinned again.

Orla hated to admit it, but she was starting to like this foxy woman. She shrugged. "Well then."

Mori said nothing further, shifting back into a fox effortlessly. She stared at the group of men.

The mooks were charging now, showering their sparks of power all around them, showing off. Orla growled under her breath, and from the corner of her eyes, she saw Lorcan carrying Chiyo, still unconscious, toward the back of the pillar.

The attackers' clothes all had a symbol, and it stood to reason that this was to show that they were members of the Yakuz group.

"The girl! Get the girl!" They mangled the words in English. Orla wanted to throw her hands over her ears because the voice was so gravelly that it almost hurt to listen. "Give us the girl, and we'll let the rest of you leave here in one piece."

"There were three ladies here, actually—one alive, one unconscious, and a female fox. Which one do you want?" Orla asked.

Orla put herself between the group of criminals that now blocked the only way into and out of the temple and the unconscious doctor who had been half hidden under the altar. She could see that Lorcan had moved to where he could protect Chiyo and still fight if it came to that. The little red fox stood somewhere between Orla and Lorcan, glaring at the gang in defiance. One figure at the back of the group stood out. It was taller and dressed more elaborately than the rest. Orla took this to mean that he was the leader. With a wave of his hand, he sent his minions out to fight his battle.

It was a fight between her magic, fireballs and whatever weapons the goons had with them. She used the last reserves of dark magic that she had to blind the ones in front of them, making it so they could only see the horrors of their past. The three that she was fighting turned and ran blindly out of the temple. She didn't have a second to take a breath before another figure loomed in front of her. This one would have to be handled the old-fashioned way, with fists. It got a strong punch in to her face, and her head snapped back. She shook her head to clear it then came at him with all the fury she possessed. It was like Orla had turned into a wild cat, hissing and clawing her way through its protective clothing to the flesh underneath. When she finally had the joy of seeing her opponent run, she turned to look at Mori and Lorcan.

Lorcan had a few cuts and bruises, but with his new unexplained ability to heal himself, she wasn't too worried about him. Mori had a large gash in her tail, but she seemed to be fine, too. Before Orla could say anything, she saw something small whizzing towards Lorcan's chest. She whirled around to try to stop it, but Mori beat her to it. The little red fox threw herself into the air, was knocked backwards as the object hit her, then fell to the cracked and crumbling cobblestones, shaking.

Orla turned to face the now empty doorway, looking for a target to let her anger and aggression out on, but finding none. When she turned to face the wounded fox, the animal was gone, and the woman stood in its place. Lorcan was reaching out to her, but she only stumbled away, trying to run, but only managing to zigzag dangerously.

"What just happened?" Orla was stunned and wasn't quite sure that she believed her own eyes, so she looked to Lorcan for confirmation.

"One of the bastards shot at me. She copped the bullet." Then he darted after Mori.

"Lorcan!" Orla called out. A wounded little fox and an injured man didn't make a good pack. Orla chased after him.

It was dark outside, and the blood trail Mori left was not easy to find. Lorcan ran and ran. Orla was right behind him. *A wounded fox can't run that fast, can she?* Lorcan asked himself. He didn't think much as he followed, but he actually sniffed the air for a scent of Mori. He followed the faint trace of her in the air, which led him straight to a spot on the road where there was a small pool of blood.

Lorcan crouched and sniffed the air again. Then he looked down at his arm and saw his skin glowing blue for a brief second. He jumped back to his feet and cursed. He didn't like this at all. Orla had caught up, out of breath. They walked a little farther and stopped where the blood trail completely disappeared.

CHAPTER 20

From a distance, Mori could see Lorcan and Orla walk away. She had been watching Lorcan—the way he went after her, the way he sniffed the air, trying to detect her scent, and the determination in his eyes. She knew he wasn't an ordinary human, but as to what he actually was, she didn't know. Mori didn't know how to explain her feelings, but what had been developing in her the last few days was disconcerting. She rubbed at the bullet wound which was still bleeding. She didn't know why she had taken the bullet. She wasn't invincible. If she died for this stranger, that meant she would have abandoned her mission and failed her ancestors and her family.

She peeked her head out, and when she saw that Lorcan and Orla had turned the corner, she limped out. She hadn't walked two steps when she heard a low growl that prickled all of her senses. She knew she was in trouble. Behind her were three gigantic wolves from a clan she had chased away a couple of years ago. She knew they held a grudge, but they had never come close to attacking her. Mori staggered back and shifted into her fox form, a tiny red fox against three large menacing wolves.

The wolves charged at her, teeth bared. For a bystander, this would just look like a dog fight. They charged at Mori. Her clan were too far away to call. If she were to go down now, she would put up a good fight. She lowered her front legs, crouched in a fighting stance, and waited. The wolves came in a whirl of dirt and stone and a wall of howling sound. She was bitten everywhere, but she was sure each of the wolves received their fair share of her teeth.

The bullet in her body was damn inconvenient. The pain slowed her down. She staggered, fell, and got bitten more. She was sure she'd be turned into a pile of bloody meat soon. Then a familiar howl came—that was Roy. The relief made her delirious.

She could rest now, she might just lie down for a bit. Mori felt her eyes droop and the energy drain out of her. Then everything was a blur.

She woke to find herself in the backseat of a car. She sat up, groggily, feeling a faint pain in her stomach where the bullet used to be. Her body must have pushed it out, and the wound was healing. She glanced up at the rearview mirror at the front seat of the car and saw Roy's intent eyes looking at her. "Thank you," she said.

"You should lie down." Roy said nothing else and focused his eyes on the road ahead. He was her guard. As a human, he owned a construction business in town. As a were-creature, he had mixed fox and wolf blood. Although he considered himself more of a fox than a wolf, because of his mixed blood, he could never be the male Alpha of the group regardless of how dominant he was or the fact that his father had been the previous alpha in the fox clan. Roy didn't complain—he didn't want the responsibility anyway. He hung around the group a lot because of Mori. He protected her and would always be there when she needed him, with the understanding that she could never mate with him.

"I see that you can't help but manage to put yourself in harm's way."

"Why would I intentionally harm myself?"

"If you'd stay where you're supposed to stay, then nothing would happen. And what's with the bullet wound? What if that bullet had been in your head? There would be nothing I could do to save you. I don't think you put the best interests of your clan at the top of your mind. That's fine, I couldn't care less. But if you die, your clan will be left in chaos, and your people will die. Is that what you want? If I stayed out of town a little longer, would I come back and have to attend your funeral?" His voice exploded with anger.

"I didn't plan this. It was the Yakuz."

Roy hit the brakes, and the car swung and stopped at the side of the road. In the mirror, Mori could see the fury in his darkened eyes. Long strands of hair flopped down onto his forehead, making his long, lean face more mysterious and, she had to admit, beautiful.

The Yakuz had killed his parents. Roy didn't want to be involved in the clan's politics and had said he would not seek revenge for his parents' deaths, but the hatred was ingrained in him, and it soared when his mental shield was weakened. Mori knew him. She could read his mind as if it was the palm of her hand. He cared for her, and at the moment, his anger at her injuries had weakened his mind. She was responsible for fueling it. She wanted him to be at peace, and the only way to achieve that was for him to seek revenge. That was her way. She was the female alpha after all, and he was her guard.

"The Yakuz are after the key again. I don't know what triggered them, but I had to stop them before they came right to our doorstep." Mori's voice was soothing.

Roy nodded and shrugged in agreement. He put the hand brake on, raked his hand through his hair, and leaned back in his seat with his eyes closed.

"There are two strangers from out of town. They're after the key as well, but I don't think they mean any harm. I think they could help us."

"How so?"

"Well, if they really are good people, and they can take the key to a safe place far away from here and protect it, it will be an enormous load off our shoulders."

"But how can we be sure they're good people?"

Mori shrugged. "I guess that's the problem. But at the moment, they could use some help. And . . . and . . . there is a thing . . . I think I bit a were-creature."

Roy's eyes flung wide open, making Mori cringe and want to sink into the car seat. "You did what?

You bit or you didn't bite? What does that mean by you *think* you bit a creature?"

Mori waved her arms in defense. "I thought he was human. I *still* think he's human, just his blood didn't taste human. The bite wasn't intentional."

Roy cracked up. "You know what, I think the biting ritual is rubbish, okay? So, I don't care if it was intentional or not. It means nothing to me. But the simple truth is, if you open your mouth, use the strength of your jaw muscles, aim, and sink your teeth into someone's flesh until it bleeds, you can't say it was unintentional!"

Mori shrugged. "Just wanted to let you know."

"Why?"

"Nothing."

"Ah. So I guess you bit the from-out-of-towner?"

She nodded.

"Was he severely hurt?"

"Not because of the bite."

Roy cocked an eyebrow.

"I kinda threw a knife at him as well, and his girlfriend helped with a fire ball. But don't worry— he's completely healed from his injuries now. Plus, I copped a bullet for him, so we're even."

"Right."

"Oh, and the Palm-eye spy we placed in the Yakuz, he's dead now. So we've lost that lead. Our only lead. The Yakuz kidnapped Chiyo and killed her boyfriend."

Roy leaned his forehead on the steering wheel. "Do you need more time to write a list of all the unfortunate events that occurred when I was out of town for less than a week?"

"No. That's it."

CHAPTER 21

Lorcan and Orla returned to the warehouse after chasing Mori, and found Chiyo had regained consciousness. They shouldn't have left her alone to chase the werefox, but they did, and it was a relief to see that she was fine. She sat next to the Goro's body. Lorcan helped her to her feet, and she wobbled a little. Her face was cold, and tears still fell from her eyes intermittently, but that was something neither Orla nor Lorcan could help her with. Not many people had to watch a loved one executed right before their eyes—that was a traumatic experience that would never go away.

The young doctor allowed herself to be led home, and she didn't speak until they got there. Even though Orla and Lorcan stumbled a bit, trying to make their way back to her house, she didn't help them. For the first time, Orla felt a kinship to her. She knew what it was like to lose someone she loved. Lorcan had died twice, but she'd been able to bring him back. Chiyo didn't have the power to do that for Goro. Even if she did, now that Goro had been dead for a while, there was no telling what he would come back as.

"I don't understand." They were the first words Chiyo had spoken since she'd come to, and they startled Orla and Lorcan. "How could I have been so vulnerable? I've depended on the two of you for my safety and protection. I'm embarrassed that I couldn't do it for myself. And for Goro." She fell silent as the name passed her lips. Whether she wanted them to be sympathetic to her or not, Lorcan and Orla couldn't tell, and they remained silent instead.

Orla and Lorcan looked around the house to check for signs of intruders. The body of the man with the eye on his hand was gone. Orla had been right. The Yakuz had come straight to Chiyo's house, looking for them. They'd barely gotten away with their lives last time, and they were both still worried about Mori, who'd taken a bullet for Lorcan.

"It's not your fault." The silence had gotten to Orla, and she wanted to break it. "You had no idea what you were dealing with, and even if you had, would you have believed it was happening?" The gentle tone with which Orla addressed Chiyo surprised Lorcan, and he raised an eyebrow. Orla scowled at him and turned back to Chiyo, who was now shaking her head.

"No, I guess I wouldn't have. You're right. But how could I have been so blind?" Chiyo, her head down, was now making her way to the kitchen table, and when she reached it, she sat down and lay her head on her arms. She looked so broken and lonely that Orla wanted to put her arms around the woman in comfort, but she didn't trust her completely. Just because they were protecting her didn't mean she would necessarily play nice in the schoolyard.

Lorcan sat on the other side of the young doctor and put a hand gently on her arm. "I don't know if it's a good idea for you to stay in this house. They obviously know where you live, and they could send more monsters after you when we're not here to protect you. Is there somewhere else you could go for a little while?" Lorcan tried to make the possibility of more trouble seem less likely than it was.

Silence ensued for a few minutes, then Chiyo raised her head. Her eyes were blank and staring, but she said, "I need you to take me to see someone."

When she didn't elaborate after a few minutes, Orla became impatient. "Okay, and who is this person? Someone you can stay with? Someone who can protect you? Can you give us a little more to go on?" Lorcan hid his smile. He'd been worried about her for a little while, but it looked like she was back to her normal self now.

"He's an old man who lives on the edge of the village. He used to be good friends with my grandfather. He might even know something about the Rojin and this key that everyone's trying to get their hands on." Chiyo shrugged innocently.

Orla jumped to her feet. "Why are you just telling us about him now? Why didn't you help us find him when we first came to you?" Anger blazed in her eyes, and as far as Lorcan could tell, she was ready to do battle. He positioned himself on the edge of his chair, just in case he had to dive between the two women.

"I thought you were Yakuz at first. After that, well, there really hasn't been time, has there?" Chiyo's voice was almost dreamlike. Grief did strange things to people, that was something that Lorcan knew about first hand.

"Okay, let's say for argument's sake that we take you to see this old man. Then what?" Orla asked.

Chiyo shrugged again. "He might be able to help you. He claims to be a wizard, and he's the last remaining member of the Rojin group. He might know about that key you were asking me about. It seems like everyone wants the damn thing now." The last part she mumbled more to herself than to her audience, but they heard her just the same.

"Do you know how to find this wizard? I assume he's within a walkable distance?" Despite her best efforts, Orla couldn't keep the sarcasm out of her voice. Chiyo turned to face them again and nodded. She didn't seem at all aware of the growing tension in her new friends. "Then let's go. I want to see if he knows anything, and the sooner the better."

CHAPTER 22

Silently, Chiyo led the group through the winding roads of the city. Now that it was early morning, traffic was picking up, and the streets were considerably more crowded. Orla and Lorcan kept their eyes darting everywhere—they couldn't afford another attack. The walk took them just over two hours, but they arrived at a little hut on the outskirts of the village that looked like it might have grown out of the earth. There was a heavy metallic scent in the air around it, and Orla thought it had to be another breed of magic. Chiyo squared her shoulders and marched right up to the front door, hesitating only slightly before giving the old wood a sound beating. She retreated a few paces, trying to appear less of a threat. As they waited, a chill crept down Orla's spine. She sidestepped, moving a little closer to Lorcan, muttering under her breath, "Something's not right." Lorcan looked around, tense and on edge, but he didn't see anything alarming.

"What do you mean?" The whispered conversation wasn't meant for Chiyo's ears, and since she hadn't turned around, they were safe in assuming that she hadn't heard them.

"I just get his feeling that something's off about Chiyo. I can't put my finger on it, but I feel a wrongness."

Lorcan shrugged. "Her boyfriend's throat was cut right in front of her, I'm surprised she didn't go mad. It's to be expected that she's behaving a little oddly."

"I'm telling you that from a magical standpoint, something is off. I just don't know what." She huffed as she stepped further away from him. Lorcan was going to make a smart remark back to her, but at that moment, the door opened, and a stooped, wizened old man came out.

"Can I help you?" The old man opened the door wide. Chiyo took a step forward and began speaking hurriedly in Japanese. The old man listened politely, and when her river of words dried up, Chiyo fell silent, waiting. The man looked over her shoulders at Orla and Lorcan. Then he looked at her, focused. He had a genuine and calm smile. He said something, and she looked up at him. It felt like the warm reunion of very familiar acquaintances. In Western culture, people would jump up and down, embracing each other in joy and tears. But here, it was expressed in polite nods and bows.

The old man said nothing to Lorcan and Orla, but motioned them to come into his hut as well. Orla wondered if he knew the concept of robbery, or if a stranger had ever pulled a weapon on him. Maybe not, judging by the way he enthusiastically ushered them into his home. The man waited patiently for them to come into his kitchen before he closed and bolted the door behind them. "Please, sit down. We have much to talk about." The trio of visitors stood awkwardly, not sure if they should do as he said, and casting furtive glances at one another. The old man sat down, then spread his arms out to encompass the other seats in another silent invitation to sit down. Chiyo was the first to obey. Orla and Lorcan followed, but they sat stiffly, ready to spring into action at a moment's notice.

"You can go ahead and relax. We're safe here as long as my wards and shields are up. I know a little of what you're going through from what Chiyo told me, but I can assure you that nothing can attack you in my house." For some reason that she couldn't explain, Orla believed him, and she sat back in her chair, keeping her hands in her lap.

"Chiyo, you have grown up a lot since the last time I saw you. I am sorry to say that I might not have the answers to all of your questions. I don't know much. But there is something I have to tell you. Are you comfortable for me to speak in front of your new friends?" the wizard asked.

Chiyo's eyes widened, and she nodded slowly. "Your father was a shape shifter." Chiyo's mouth dropped open in astonishment. "He could turn into an eagle, but only that one animal. Your mother knew all about it, of course, because she was part werefox. Her family thought that she was marrying beneath her, and they weren't happy at all with the union between them. Then they had you. You were the deadliner in their family." The old man paused, waiting for his information to sink in. Chiyo was shaking her head.

"No. My parents were normal. They had no special abilities, and they never did anything to get them noticed. I didn't even know that my mother had a family on her side."

When her words subsided, the old man spoke again. "You were to end the magical abilities in their lines. You have no powers and do not have the ability to pass any on, either."

Chiyo finally came back to herself and waved away the explanation as if she wasn't interested. She changed the topic of conversation quickly. "Now about this key. You were in the Rojin, and you were friends with my grandfather. You have to tell me what it is and where I can find it."

The wizard looked sharply into her face then crossed his arms over his chest, contemplating. He leaned back in his seat. "I'm not comfortable talking about that key, and I don't have any information to give you."

Chiyo's face clouded with anger, and she jumped to her feet. "You told me that you would answer the questions that I asked truthfully! How dare you go back on your word!" She shook an accusatory finger in the old man's face. Orla and Lorcan had both shifted a little in their chairs once she'd jumped to her feet, but they'd remained seated.

"I did tell you that I would tell you the truth, and I have about your family. I'd rather not discuss that key. If you have any other questions you need answered, I would be more than happy to tell you what I know." His tone was measured and even, but Orla could see electricity in his eyes. He might seem like a kindly old man, but she knew better than to take anything at face value when there was magic involved. He was giving Chiyo a clear warning that she wasn't heeding. Chiyo begged and pleaded, screamed and cried, but no matter what she did, the wizard wouldn't tell her anything about the key of Psuche. The trio left the wizard's house in disappointment, each with their own reasons.

"That key has to be somewhere close by! If it wasn't, he wouldn't be so secretive. If we start looking, I bet we can find it," Chiyo said and stomped ahead. Lorcan increased his pace to follow, but Orla grabbed him and shook her head.

A misty breeze whirled up from the ground, and an eerie cold wind crept out from the gaps between trees and small shrubs along the road. They were outside the remote village, and Chiyo didn't seem to be heading in the direction of civilization.

If Orla wasn't mistaken, there was a reptilian hiss hovering in the air, and she was praying that it wasn't coming from snakes. She wasn't afraid of them, but she never knew which way they were heading, and that gave her a disadvantage in combat. Lorcan heard the sound, too.

He glanced around, feeling uneasy.

CHAPTER 23

Chiyo was now suddenly bound and determined to find the key, and it made Orla uneasy. She'd been swearing up and down that she knew nothing about it and wanted nothing to do with it this whole time, but now she'd made a complete one-eighty. It was as if her personality had changed somehow, like something else was directing her body and mind without her knowledge. Encouraged by the weird aura surrounding them at the moment, Orla decided to try to pry into Chiyo's mind. This was a shady area of magic she hadn't touched since she was a kid. But it was needed now.

Unbeknownst to either of her companions, Orla began to weave her fingers in a complicated pattern, spinning dark magic in her mind for a spell. It would let her touch Chiyo's mind to see what she was really up to. It took her only a few minutes to complete the spell, and then she held her hand up to her face. The small ball of purple lightning that crackled in her palm didn't look like much, but it made Orla smile. She blew it gently in Chiyo's direction and waited. The ball of lightning spun on the air currents towards its intended target. When it reached Chiyo, it drew even with her ear and then lengthened before slowly seeping into her ear like water into a gutter.

Orla gasped and stumbled. Lorcan glanced back at her, but she gestured him to go on ahead. She regained her footing, but she still couldn't wrap her mind around what her magic was telling her was real. Chiyo's mind was empty. The ball of lightning couldn't gather any information from her because there was none to be had. Orla's body was still walking, but she was trapped now in the link between her own mind and that of Chiyo. Orla's body fell to the ground, unconscious; her path back to herself was cut off.

Hearing the sound of Orla's body thumping to the ground, Lorcan turned back. "Holy crap," he called out and darted back to her. "Chiyo," Lorcan called out for the doctor. "Please help." He shook Orla's shoulders, but her body seemed completely shut down. Lorcan was panicking. "Come on, honey. Open your eyes for me. Tell me what's going on. Chiyo!"

Silence. No response from Chiyo. Lorcan looked up.

Chiyo began to laugh, a loud, guttural sound that sounded inhuman. Chiyo's hair began to shrink upwards, like her scalp was reabsorbing it. She grew taller, and her smooth skin began to break out in bumps and ridges like that of a lizard. He watched as the creature reared back on its hind legs, returning to where Orla lay on the ground.

Lorcan sprang into action, trading blows and insults with the Godzilla wannabe in front of him. He made sure to keep himself between this creature and Orla. The more that Lorcan began to think his moves out in advance, the faster he became. His agility increased after every few moves until he was darting around like a little fox toying with a much larger predator. The lizard whipped her tail and dealt him more than just a glancing blow to his midsection. Lorcan let out a howl that didn't even register in his own mind.

Lorcan swore as he reminded himself of what Orla had whispered to him in front of the wizard's hut. She'd said something about Chiyo not being normal. That something was amiss with her now in a magical sense that hadn't been wrong before. Lorcan had thought nothing of it. He promised himself to take whatever she said about magic more seriously from now on—*if* they had a chance to move on after this. The thing in front of him was awfully big, and he didn't have a weapon. But he'd be damned, though, if he'd let this overgrown iguana harm Orla.

The lizard stomped toward Lorcan. He lunged at it with all he had. At the moment, he realized that his only weapons were his will and his fists. Punching the lizard felt like punching rusty metal panels. His knuckles tore and bled, and he swore it wasn't his imagination that the lizard grinned at him. It swung a gigantic tail at Lorcan, and he was knocked four feet, rolling and scraping against the dirt road.

The lizard then turned toward Orla. Lorcan charged at it again, and copped another blow from its tail. He reeled up, his nose bleeding, his face scratched. This wasn't smart, fighting bare-handed with the creature, he thought. But what choice did he have? The lizard was approaching Orla, and he couldn't figure out how to stop it. Fury increased inside him, boiling his blood. He grabbed a tree branch and swung at the creature. It broke the branch with its tail, and Lorcan took another hit. There was only so much his human body could take. The thought raised a wave of strange energy in him.

He needed something heavier. He saw a large rock on the ground. When he reached to pick it up, his hands—or what used to be his hands—were now paws at the end of hairy electric blue animal legs. He turned to look at the lizard, and his vision was strange, rounded with blurry edges, and his viewpoint seemed to be very low to the ground. He was totally confused. He wanted to move forward but found himself tangled in his clothing. He shrugged off his jeans and shirt and lunged at the lizard. He wanted to grunt, but the sound erupting from his mouth was not a grunt, it was a howl.

The lizard turned around, paying him some attention now. It waved its tail and thumped it on the ground, sounding almost like the rumble of a small earthquake. Lorcan walked around, circling the lizard. He realized he was walking on all fours now, and admittedly, he felt comfortable and very agile. He wanted to say something, but the words wouldn't come out of his mouth. He jumped at the lizard, climbed up its back from its tail and over the top of its head, biting down on its soft weak spot, the eye.

The lizard roared. Lorcan wagered if it were a dragon, it would have let out a stream of fire. But unfortunately for the reptile, it was merely an ugly lizard. It swung its head, hurling Lorcan to the ground. He howled in pain and then saw the lizard's foot about to crush him. Springing to his feet to get away, he felt the lizard step on his tail.

Tail? Lorcan turned to see that he had a large, furry tail. He tried to drag it out from under the lizard's foot, but it didn't seem to move. He saw another foot coming down. This might be the end of him.

PART TWO

CHAPTER 24

A blast of icy blue energy sizzled over Lorcan's head and hit the lizard square in the chest. He whipped around as the lizard began to scream in agony and saw the old wizard coming to the rescue, using his staff as a wand of some sort and shooting out blasts of energy from the tip. A final blast threw the overgrown lizard back about ten yards before it collapsed and lay still.

The wizard turned, looked at Lorcan, and gave him a warm smile. "It's a shape shifter. Just like you. But it's gone now, you needn't worry."

Lorcan was still standing protectively in front of Orla's immobile form, but he couldn't lift her up with his paws. The wizard crouched down next to him, "If this is your first time, it must be hard for you."

Lorcan felt lightheaded. He staggered away, stumbling as his limbs stretched out unexpectedly. He lay down on the ground, gripping the earth for balance as his world seemed to spin out of its orbit. He looked down to see his human hands grabbing the dirt, and then he blacked out for a brief moment. When he awakened, Lorcan sprang to his feet, shivering in the cold. He looked down and saw he was completely naked. He dashed to the pile of clothes he'd shed earlier and put them on.

The wizard smiled and waited patiently. He then knelt at Orla's side. He murmured some words and ran his hands the length of her body, pushing a green energy into her. Orla's eyes snapped open, and she gasped. Sitting up hurriedly, her chest heaved in fear. Lorcan gathered her up into his arms. He crooned to her, calming her down until she stopped trembling.

"If you could learn to control your dark magic, child, you could be very powerful indeed," the wizard said.

Orla stared at him, not knowing how he'd gotten here or what he was talking about. "What do you mean?" she asked groggily.

He smiled at her like a kindly old grandfather. "I'm familiar with your branch of sorcery, dear, and if you could refine the use of your powers, you could be quite formidable. If you'd like, I can try to teach you." Orla looked from him to Lorcan and back again. The old man nodded, understanding that she make her decision later. "As for you, son, what happened was powerful. Use it to your advantage. You need to practice and see what works best for you."

Lorcan said nothing in response.

The wizard nodded. "I'm sure both of you need some time to adjust, make sense of what just happened, and discover your natural talent. Come to me if you need help. Remember, things like this happen for a reason. Don't take it for granted."

The wizard smiled, stood, and walked quickly away in the direction from which he'd come.

"What was he talking about?" Orla asked.

"You passed out, and Chiyo turned into a gigantic lizard that I had to fight off."

"What?" Orla sat up and saw the dead creature. She got up to her feet and inched toward it. "That's why its head was empty."

"What?" Lorcan asked.

"I was attempting to get into Chiyo's—I mean, the lizard's—head. I think it must have figured it out."

"Are you saying you used your magic without telling me?"

"There wasn't time to tell you. How did you fight this huge animal with your bare hands?"

"Well, it wasn't me who killed it. It was the old man with his magic."

"What was he talking about? Your talent? I know you're a good fighter, but it sounded like he was referring to something else completely."

"Well, I turned myself into a dragon, flew fifty feet into the air, threw jets of fire at the lizard, and killed it in one go. How does that sound?"

She smiled. "Not funny."

Lorcan pulled her into his arms. "I know it's not, but please laugh anyway." When she pasted an awkward grin on her face, he shook his head. "That look could scare little children." He embraced her tightly and kissed her forehead, his body shuddering with emotion. He knew she could feel it. The moment he'd seen his paws and felt that he couldn't protect her, couldn't speak, couldn't call out for her—the helplessness of that moment came back to him now in a blast of emotions.

Looking up at Lorcan, Orla stared into his eyes and felt like she could lose herself in them for the rest of eternity. "Thank you," she said.

"I didn't exactly . . ." She stopped his words with her kiss.

They stood in the chill air for a while, then reality came flooding back. "Lorcan, I don't think the Chiyo-lizard that attacked us was the real Chiyo. I know you won't believe me, but I feel like there was something different about her. My magic picked up on it when she was knocking on the old man's door. Something different about her presence."

"Then we should ask the wizard for his opinion. Also, I think you should take him up on his offer."

"What offer?"

"To teach you how to control your dark magic."

Orla raised her arms. "You think I can't control my magic?"

Lorcan grabbed her arms. "No, please. I can't handle two episodes from you in a day."

CHAPTER 25

The pack gathered at their secret meeting place at a small temple on top of the hill. Mori walked in, Roy flanking her right side. There were twenty other werefoxes around, now in human form. Mori sensed a strange aura in the air, but said nothing. As usual, she walked to the middle of the room as the leader of the group. Five senior members of the clan sat on chairs on a raised platform in a corner of the temple.

Roy glanced at Mori to be sure she was okay. She limped a bit but seemed to be moving fine. Mori looked up and caught his deep brown eyes—

her fierce gaze always made any other fox flinch, but not him. He smiled at her instead.

An old man standing at a corner grumbled, "Why was this meeting so urgent? I need to work for a living. If you can't bring in the money to support us, at least give us some room to maneuver. You can't expect us to drop everything to be here on a whim."

"This is urgent." Mori gave him a stern stare. "Don't speak before I do. And don't speculate on whether or not it's important. The clan's matters come first and are of utmost priority. If you can't make a living doing what you're doing, the clan will support you financially, but you have to earn your way first."

Everybody turned to look at the old man. He stared back at them, shoving his hands into his pockets and casting a condescending look on Mori. She ignored him and spoke slowly and clearly, "The Yakuz were looking for the key again." She waited for few seconds, letting the information sink in while she gauged the reactions of the senior members. The five sitting on chairs looked at one another.

"What proof do you have of that?" one of them asked.

"I know someone in town who might have information about the key and its location. This person was attacked, kidnapped, and tortured for the information. Our spy in the Yakuz was killed during the process," she answered.

"The Yakuz!" There were rumblings among the people in the temple. They looked at one another. Amid the confusion, Mori knew, there was fear. It wasn't the Yakuz, but the fear that worked to destroy the morality of her clan. It was her worst nightmare.

She projected her voice to the far end of the room. "And before you ask, I don't know what triggered the attack. I don't know why they want the key . . . or why now. But it's our mission to protect it and the secrets that come with it, so we must delegate more members to the location—just in case they find out where it is and decide to hunt for it."

The old man who spoke before raised his voice. "Are you saying you want to send our people to that place? Are they supposed to remain there for the rest of their lives? I, for one, am not volunteering for this."

"And I'm not asking for volunteers." Mori stared at him, demanding his silence. "As I said before, I don't know what triggered the Yakuz attack. But war is coming our way, and we have to live up to our sacred mission."

"We've sacrificed enough for the mission," said one of the senior members.

"What do you mean?" Mori asked him.

"You are too young to know. I have seen deaths. I've seen the battle, and I think we've given enough," the old man muttered.

"What are you talking about?" asked a young member on the floor.

The crowd fired up with questions, and Mori didn't know which one to answer first.

Sai, a man in his mid-twenties, stepped out to the middle of the room. He had inherited his family's fortune and was willing to throw money at anything that money could buy. The only thing he didn't have to go along with his wealth was the alpha bloodline. "The Yakuz are deadly. You ask us to protect the key, but what do you do to protect us, Mori?" he asked, broaching a sensitive topic. Everyone quieted, allowing Mori to answer.

"I'll handle this. I'll negotiate with the Mahito family. They've been supporting us for generations," Mori responded.

"You are too young and inexperienced to handle this," said a senior member. "I can help with the negotiation. I've established good rapport with the Mahitos," said another senior member.

Mori smiled, but Sai jumped in and cut her smile short. "She's the alpha—she should be negotiating. The Mahitos are outsiders. They don't understand fox business. If you need money, you have only to ask me," he grinned. "But money isn't going to buy back our long lost power in the werefox world, will not buy back the lives we have lost protecting the key."

Mori narrowed her eyes. "What are you proposing?"

"I want to protect this clan. I want everyone to be safe. And I can do it for real. Not just talk. We don't work for nothing. Guarding the stupid key is equal to working for nothing, and I don't like that." Sai paced, circling Mori, looking her up and down. He moved a step closer but then felt Roy's hand on his shoulder, gripping him like a pair of iron pliers. Sai glanced up and gauged Roy's eyes, eyes that looked as if they could shoot fire at Sai. He knew he'd be at a disadvantage against Roy, so he withdrew.

"No, we don't want to do this. Whatever it was, the mission began before our time. Now we have families to take care of," a middle-aged man added from the far end of the room.

His comment triggered a round of similar protests.

"We won't honor this mission."

"We've done our fair share."

"If I can't protect my family, what the hell am I doing protecting a mysterious key?"

Mori raised her voice over them. "But you know what will happen to the city if the key lands in the wrong hands. We'll all die. You family's survival is a moot point in a dead city."

Silence. Just when the crowd seemed to be on the verge of agreeing with Mori, Sai spoke again. "Yes, the key protects the city and keeps it safe. But it's been our responsibility for such a long time. We've given more than enough. It should be someone else's turn now. If the Yakuz want the key, let them have it. They won't destroy the city in which they live. They'll protect the key and stop attacking us. It's a win-win solution."

"You want to give the key to the Yakuz?" Mori stared hard at Sai. She smiled as the pieces started to come together for her. "What's in it for you, Sai?"

"As I said, I act only on the best interests of our clan."

"So you think it's best if I give up the location of the key to the Yakuz? That way, we don't have to fight?"

Sai nodded enthusiastically.

"Do you want to be the leader of the clan, Sai?"

He shrugged and said nothing.

Mori smiled. "I was wondering how the Yakuz found out about the family who knows the secret of the key. How they'd known my whereabouts that night and where I sent our spy. I also wondered how the gray wolf clan knew when I was alone and injured so they could attack me."

As Mori advanced, Sai staggered backward. "Don't you accuse me of anything! I challenge your leadership!" Sai growled.

"Challenge my leadership?"

"Yes, I'll fight for it. The old-fashioned way. If I win, I lead."

"And if you lose?"

"I'll spend the rest of my pitiful life guarding the stupid key."

There were rumbles in the room.

"No, this is not a good time for it."

"I'm supporting Mori. She's been a good leader. I don't want a fight."

"If you don't want to fight, go elsewhere."

"An alpha has to be able to defend her position in battle."

"Battle my ass, it was ancient."

A wave of arguments. People talking over one another.

Mori and Sai circled threateningly, looking into each other's eyes, about to fight.

A senior member raised his hands. "Stop this. Stop. Do not fight."

"This is tradition. If she insists we follow tradition and protect the key, then she should defend her leadership," Sai snarled, shifting into a formidable fox.

Roy darted over, grabbing Mori's hand before she shifted. "You don't have to do this. Please don't, Mori."

"I don't want to fight. But this is a leadership challenge, not a threat. You can't protect me from this, Roy." And then she shifted.

The crowd got excited now. "Fight! Fight! Fight!" they cheered.

Mori and Sai charged at each other. Mori's supporters argued with Sai's. The observers began to shift and fight amongst each other. The inside of the temple was a blur of dust, flying objects, and the sounds of wounded dog howls.

"Stop!" Roy yelled but nobody was listening. "Stop this!" he yelled again, but it made no difference. He pulled a gun and fired into the air. Silence ensued, but Sai and Mori were still snarling at each other. Both were badly injured. Blood was everywhere. Roy said nothing further, but walked to the middle of the room, snatched fox-Mori up, and swung her over his shoulders. She passed out.

Sai growled, and Roy pointed the gun at him. "Between your teeth and my gun, my money's on the gun. To all of you—I've had enough of this nonsense. You want to shift, then shift. You want to bark, fight, and kill one another, that's your problem. I'm taking Mori out of here." Roy turned on his heel and exited the temple with Mori on his shoulders.

Halfway down the hill, Mori opened her eyes, finding that she had shifted back to her human form and was dangling from Roy's shoulders. "Let me down, let me down!" Roy didn't stop. "Let me down, Roy."

"I just saved you."

"Saved my ass."

"Yes, and that, too." Roy kept walking, ignoring Mori's wriggling and verbal abuse.

CHAPTER 26

Orla and Lorcan went back to the warehouse to look for a sign of the real Chiyo and found nothing. Not only they could they not find Chiyo, but Goro's body had disappeared as well. The building was empty, save for the eerie chilled air that filled the place. They decided to go back to the wizard for more information. The old man greeted them at the door with a warm smile as if not surprised that they had come back to find him.

He made them tea, then brought the steaming cups over to the table as he settled in for a long tale. Lorcan began their story with finding the kitsune that had brought them to Chiyo's front door. From there, Orla related how Chiyo had kicked them out and they had found the temple holding her grandfather's remains. The old wizard's eyes grew sad as they spoke about his old friend, but he didn't interrupt. They next explained what had just happened and how they'd ended up at his door. When Lorcan fell silent, they waited to hear what the old man had to say. He shook his head as he thought, silently coming up with ideas and dismissing them just as quickly. When he finally settled on one that he thought might work, he smiled and looked up at the young couple in front of him.

"When she accompanied you to my door, I sensed it might not be the Chiyo I knew, but I hadn't seen her for such a long time. I wasn't sure. I don't think she's with the Yakuz, but I think it's more likely that we'll receive bad news than good. If they'd gotten the information out of her, they wouldn't have sent in the lizard shapeshifter. Don't blame yourselves—you couldn't have known."

"The shapeshifter speculated you would have information about the key. You killed the lizard—will its group know that? Will they go after you?" Lorcan asked.

The old man looked at Lorcan and smiled. "You are both looking for the key as well."

"Yes, but we were forced to do it for reasons important only to us. We're not interested in any benefits the key would give the holder. We're not gold diggers," Orla jumped in.

"I can tell that much." The wizard gave her a fatherly smile. "But as you can see, trouble follows whomever possesses the key—or even those with a whiff of information about it. What you don't know won't hurt you."

"What does it do, really?" Lorcan asked.

"Power. The key can open the source of God's power."

"What sort of power? Energy? Magic? Knowledge?" Lorcan pressed on.

"Curiosity killed the cat, young man."

Lorcan smiled. "When we put our lives on the line for this key, we're half dead already. If we can't find the key, not only will *we* be dead, but we'll put at risk the lives of other people who depend on it."

"That's the very reason I have to do whatever it takes to keep the information to myself. The key is safe now. You need not worry. But you cannot take it with you."

"We came all this way. If you want us to go away empty handed, then can you at least give us an inkling of what this key is all about? If we—and many others—are going to die because we can't have it, can you at least let us know that our cause is nothing compared to the disaster you're protecting humankind from?" Irritation overflowed in Lorcan's voice.

The old man took a few minutes, contemplating. Then he spoke slowly. "One of the power sources that the key can control or release is the water element. That was why the sea dragon wanted it. The sea dragon wanted to flood and drown the entire city. It needs the water element to do so."

Orla's eyes widened. "Sea dragon's territory expands with the water. Of course, it would want water everywhere."

The wizard nodded. Lorcan buried his head in his hands for a while, trying to gain control over his sneer. He smiled. "Sea dragons exist in children's fairy tales. There are explanations for this. At a very basic level, tides are the rise and fall of sea levels caused by the combined effects of the gravitational forces exerted by the moon, the sun, and the rotation of the Earth. Let's say someone could somehow affect the celestial rotation and ultimately impact the orbits of the related planets. That person would create tides that would drown whole city. But I can't see why someone would want to do that . . ."

"The sea dragon. The sea dragon would want that, Lorcan," Orla explained.

"Orla!" Lorcan exclaimed.

"Had I mentioned that information comes hand in hand with trouble? It's here already."

They old wizard bolted to the door with lightning speed. Lorcan and Orla were amazed to see him move so fast. They followed him, rushing out the door.

CHAPTER 27

The wizard rushed toward a shadow along the dark road. It slithered away quickly, similar to the movement of a gigantic python. Within only a few steps, the wizard had lost sight of the spying animal. Orla and Lorcan caught up with him.

"We've lost it. What was it?" Orla asked.

"A python," the wizard answered.

"Lizard, python . . . what'll be next?" Lorcan muttered. The wizard shook his head and turned back toward the house. Lorcan stopped him on his way. "Come on, we have to do better than this. We can help you. Tell us what you need. If we leave here and the Yakuz attack you, what are you going to do?"

The old man stared at Lorcan. "I'll take the secrets to my grave."

"That won't save people's lives. I can guarantee you that we can take the key to a very safe place. No one on Earth will ever have access to it. Isn't that a better solution? Think about it. You might be able to keep certain information secret, but what if they found the key in some other way? What would you be able to do about it?" Lorcan was losing his patience when the wizard suddenly turned back.

"What is the place that you're talking about? How can you be so sure it's perfectly safe?"

Lorcan pulled out his wrist unit, put it on, and pressed a series of keys. A light beamed down from the sky, and the portal to the Daimon Gate opened. The wizard could see a glimpse of the goings-on at the entrance. Then Lorcan shut the portal and put the unit away. The wizard gasped, looking at Lorcan with a newfound respect.

"You never mentioned that you could wield magic, young man." His tone was borderline accusatory, but Lorcan just grinned at him and shrugged.

"I wouldn't call it magic, exactly. I'd just call it using my resources to get what I need. That is the place where I will keep the key safe. It's not on Earth—it's another universe. There are many worlds just like the world you live in now. The place I showed you doesn't give access to evil men from Earth. The Yakuz and the sea dragon could never get the key. Do you understand?"

The wizard hesitated.

"I'm trusting you with our lives now, and it's not the first time. Can't you trust us just a little bit? I can build a data portfolio for you about all of Japan's natural disasters. I can locate places you think the sea dragon might be. I can dig up information on the Yakuz for you. I have access to a system off-planet that can do that and more. Everything, that is, *except* magic."

The wizard looked at him for a long time, then seemed to silently consent, sinking in to himself a bit. To Orla, it looked like the old man struggled with a load too heavy for his frail shoulders to bear. He nodded, but before he could say anything further, a group of shapeshifters swooped down from the sky as hawks, attacking them with their sharp talons. Orla had the presence of mind to duck, but the old man and Lorcan had been caught unaware. Lorcan's face was gouged, and the old man was knocked over. Orla decided it was time for her to vent her anger from the close call she'd experienced at the hands of the lizard, and as these punks were obviously working for the same side as the reptile, they were fair game.

She began to chant under her breath, and purple lightning formed at her fingertips. Her eyes were open, following one bird, and then another. Once her gaze settled on one, lightning bolts flowed from her fingers, and the bird was zapped badly enough that it fell out of the sky and thought twice about trying to attack the group again. She was losing time trying to focus on one of the hawks at a time, but she was the only one who could fight them off. Lorcan had no way of getting to them, and the wizard was dazed, though valiantly trying to get back to his feet.

"You won't have to handle them alone. I'm adding my magic to yours." He let her know he was with her, and that somehow helped Orla gather her strength and courage for a major attack. She had her back to the wizard, and so she didn't see that five of the hawks were flying in carrying a net with a large boulder in it. The old man was busy chanting with his eyes closed, and Lorcan was ducking to avoid an onslaught of vicious talons. The hawks let loose, and the boulder fell . . . right onto the old man. It crushed his chest, and that drew Lorcan over to him to try to protect him as best he could while Orla killed the rest.

She was stunned by the sight she saw when she turned around, but it only served to anger her more. The bolts of lightning were now thicker and seemed to have minds of their own. She no longer had to aim for individual birds—the lightning was doing it for her.

She fell to her knees near the old man, apologizing for being watchful and asking if there was anything she could do to save him. He patted her hand. "No, child. You can't help me, but you can help by taking the key to a safe place. I have a map that will lead you to the temple. Please do it as soon as you can . . ." His body tensed, his eyes closed, and he took his last breath.

CHAPTER 28

Orla took the map from the man and unfolded it. They were, indeed, very close to the temple. But before they could determine anything further from the map, Lorcan sniffed the air. "Mori," he whispered.

"What?" Orla was astonished, not because he had spoken Mori's name but because he had sniffed the air and known it was her. He obviously didn't even realize what he was doing. "Mori," Lorcan repeated. He stood and glanced around. All of a sudden, a car raced out from a hill coming from a small road in the bush. Mori appeared to be tied up in the back seat of the car. She was kicking and shouting at the driver. The car swerved onto the main road and headed into town.

Lorcan chased the car. "Lorcan!" Orla called out. "You can't chase them on foot!" Lorcan kept sprinting. "Lorcan!" Orla called again. Lorcan stopped.

"He got Mori. Someone got her."

"I can see that, but we can't chase them on foot."

"What do you suggest?"

Orla ran to a side street. She saw a scooter parked in an empty front yard. She made a run for it, ducked down by the scooter's side, and picked the lock. It took her only a few seconds. "Sorry," she mumbled to the absent owner as she pushed the scooter away toward the corner where Lorcan waited.

"We'll return it, of course," she said when she saw the look on Lorcan's face.

"Do you know how to drive one of these?" he asked.

"Can't be more difficult than riding a horse."

"It is. A horse has four legs and can stand by itself."

She shrugged. "You want to get Mori, here's your chance."

Lorcan looked at the vehicle, considered his options, and then hopped on.

"Are you sure?" Orla asked.

"There's no other way. It can't be more difficult than riding a horse, as you said."

Orla grinned and hopped on.

When they were on the road heading into town, Orla noticed Lorcan sniffing the air repeatedly for Mori's scent.

"Do you realize that you're sniffing the air?" Orla asked.

"What?"

"Obviously not. Never mind."

***

In town—Orla called it a town, but it was actually much smaller than a village in England—they stopped in front of a small traditional Japanese house. Wrapped in manicured gardens, it was quiet and peaceful, as was the street. Orla and Lorcan surveyed the area from a hidden position around the corner.

"How do you know she'll be here?"

Lorcan shrugged, "I just know."

Shortly, the car they had seen at the village approached and parked in front of the house. From inside, a man exited, a grocery bag in one hand. Lorcan charged at him from across the street. Without speaking a single word, Lorcan landed a punch on the man's face. The groceries fell to the ground. The two men pummeled each other.

Orla helped Mori from the backseat and realized she wasn't tied up. She moved stiffly, though. "Are you okay?" Orla asked. "Don't worry, we're here . . ." she said, but stopped when she saw the worried look on Mori's face when she saw the men fighting.

"Stop fighting! Stop that! Stop!" Mori cried out.

The men ignored her and continued fighting. Orla grabbed a load of bread lying on the ground and whacked at the two men. "Stop fighting!" Orla yelled. They stopped, but they were still snarling and swearing at each other.

"You get off her," Lorcan growled.

"What the fuck!" The man ran at Lorcan again, but Orla jumped in front of him.

"Hold on. Hold on. She's all right," Orla said to Lorcan.

Lorcan turned to Mori. "Are you okay, Mori?"

Mori gingerly pressed her palm into the injuries she'd sustained in the fight with Sai. "I'm all right. It's not his fault. I'm not hurt . . . much. He was just trying to help me, Lorcan. That's Roy."

"Yes, finally, thank you!" Roy punctuated every word like a curse. "I was just trying to help." Roy paced back and forth, looking as if he needed something to punch.

Mori couldn't move quickly—she leaned against the car. "I'm sorry, Roy. Don't get mad at me." A tear dropped down onto her cheek.

Roy was astonished, and his fury evaporated into thin air like smoke. He'd never seen Mori's tears before. A woman like this didn't cry easily, and when she did, she could deflate a man's gigantic ego, Orla thought.

Roy darted over to Mori, taking her arm. "Please don't cry. Let me take you inside."

"Would you like to come in?" Mori asked Lorcan and Orla.

Lorcan was about to refuse, but Orla chimed in with an agreement before he could utter a word.

CHAPTER 29

That night, Orla and Lorcan stayed in the guest room of Roy's house. Snuggling on the futon, Orla toyed with a strand of hair on Lorcan's face and looked into his striking blue eyes. He smiled at her. "We haven't had a proper wedding yet. I'm sorry." He smoothed her hair and pulled her into his arms.

"The wedding is just a formality. You haven't proposed properly."

He hopped up on his elbows. "I did, in London." She lay down on her arm. "Really? I can't seem to recall."

"That's all right. I'll do it all over again." He inched closer to her, and his hands began to get very busy on her body. Some nibbling here, some kisses there, gentle touches in other places. Her man knew how to please a woman, Orla thought. Soon, their bodies tangled in the sheet as they drove each other to the peak of satisfaction.

***

Orla's biological clock had adjusted to the time difference. She woke naturally in the morning, but not Lorcan. He was a sleepyhead regardless of the planet he was on. She snuggled into his chest for some of his familiar warmth, thinking of another round of activity to lift the morning mood. Then she gasped and bolted out from under the blanket and off the futon, landing on her backside and dragging herself backward on the floor.

Lorcan sat up. He intended to ask if she was okay, but what came out of his mouth was a woof.

Backed against the wall, Orla calmed down instantly as she registered what had happened. "Shhhh, it's okay, Lorcan." She smiled as graciously as possible. "You see, it's okay. I'm okay," she repeated herself. In front of her was a magnificent electric blue fox. She recognized his eyes, and she could tell he was in a panic. It was not the time for her to freak out. She smiled again.

She could tell he was totally confused.

He whirled around, walking back and forth, making a pitiful little moaning sound. She inched toward him. He sat down on the futon. She reached out her hand and touched the soft fur on his head. He shook her hand off his head. As he turned around, he saw his bushy blue tail. He sprang up to all fours, jumped off the futon, and landed on the floor in front of the mirror. There, he saw it. In the mirror was a large blue fox. He snarled at himself.

"No, no, Lorcan, it's okay. We'll figure out how to handle this." Orla reached over to him, but he bolted out the door and outside to the garden.

"Lorcan!" she cried out and ran after him.

He was too fast. He disappeared into the bush. Tears streamed down her face. Orla ran back into the house. Her scream woke Mori and Roy. She stuttered so much they couldn't understand what she was saying. Eventually, she summoned all of her strength and put the words together. "Lorcan turned into a blue fox. He was totally confused, and he just ran off into the bush." And that was all she could say. She cried.

"He didn't know?" Mori asked.

Orla shook her head. The thought of losing him forever tore at her heart. Roy said nothing. He shifted into a large black fox and ran out the door.

Mori sat Orla down. Orla didn't know what to say, what to feel. *Would he come back to her? He turned in to a fox, and so what?* Orla concentrated on the current situation, and sketched a scenario in her mind. *What if she turned into an animal? What would it feel like? What would she think of herself?*

Then it dawned on her what Lorcan might feel, and the realization wasn't pleasant. But if he truly felt that way, feel like an animal and that she might leave him because of that, as long as he came back, she would change his mind.

That was, if he came back.

CHAPTER 30

It had turned dark before Roy made it home. He walked into the house, gloriously naked with fox-Lorcan on his shoulders. He walked straight into the guest room and threw fox-Lorcan down on the futon. His blue fur was soaked with wet patches of blood, his left eyelid was torn, his right ear bled, and he was apparently not conscious.

"Oh my God, what happened to him?" Orla asked in panic.

"I beat him up. Stubborn son of a bitch. He'll heal fast. You don't need to worry," Roy said.

Mori came in with a medical kit. She gave it to Orla, and then took a few bandages out and fussed over Roy's injuries. It looked as if Lorcan had put up a good fight. Mori took Roy back to his room.

Orla cleaned up all the mud and blood on Lorcan, literally from head to tail. She smoothed his magnificent blue fur. She had never seen such a beautiful animal. The thing was, he was all hers. A little later, Orla found Roy and Mori sitting in the living room. Mori poured Orla a cup of hot tea.

Sitting on the sofa, her hands still shaky, Orla couldn't make sense of the whole thing.

"He's different. I think he's a mix." Roy broke the silence.

"Like you? Fox-wolf?" Mori asked.

Roy shook his head. "I don't know. You're right, Mori, his blood tastes very strange."

Orla followed every single word in Roy and Mori's conversation, wanting to gather as much information as possible about were creatures so she could understand Lorcan better.

"How come he didn't know? Were blood is genetic. Unless he's a dead-liner who could live his whole life not knowing. But it's obvious he can shift. He can't be a dead-liner. In that case, he had to have been shifting since he was a kid. How could he live his whole life not knowing?" Roy asked.

"The other day, after Mori bit him, I think things started to change. I don't think he knew. I don't know his family, but I really don't think he knew about this ability."

"It doesn't look like he's taking it well," Mori commented.

"But were blood is, well, blood. You have it, or you don't. It's not a thing you can trigger," Roy said. The conversation continued, Mori and Roy discussing what they would do if they weren't werefoxes.

People always wanted things they couldn't have, Orla thought. She finished the tea, excused herself to go back to the guest room with Lorcan. Before she left, she asked, "When do you think he'll be able to shift back to his human form?"

"We can't speak for Lorcan, but we shift whenever we want," Mori said. "The only time I was forced was when I bit him." Orla nodded and left to be with Lorcan.

During the night, she snuggled next to Lorcan, stroking his fur and whispering into his ears that she loved him. She knew he heard her. Then she fell asleep. She felt his warm rough tongue on her cheek as she slept. She smiled at the feeling, but it might have been just a dream.

When she woke the next morning, Lorcan was still in fox form. He opened his eyes and looked at her. He stared right through her, then he closed his eyes again. She lay down next to him, stroking his fur, but he turned his head away from her. "All right, if you just want to lie here, I'll lie with you." She lay down again next to him. Then she started talking about different things, about the time they were in London and the time when she left home and he didn't find her until three years later, and what she did in between.

Hours passed, and she kept talking. She cried, she got tired, she fell asleep, she woke, and she kept talking. Still, Lorcan just lay there in his fox form. In the evening, Mori came in. "Orla, you've got to come out and eat something. You look worse than he does."

"If he wants to do this, I'll do it with him," Orla said as a tear rolled down her face.

"I'll give you tonight. But by tomorrow morning, if you guys aren't up, I'm throwing you out. You're not going to die and rot in my house," Roy said from the doorway.

When Roy and Mori had left the room, Orla reached over, pulled fox-Lorcan into her arms, and cuddled. "Well, one more night, and then we'll have to die on the street. If that's what you want." Still no sign of a response from Lorcan. She lay there for a little longer, and then she got up.

Orla went to Lorcan's computer bag and pulled out the pouch in which he kept his lucky little love stone. The yellow stone stared back at her, both encouraging and daring her. She palmed the stone and went back to Lorcan at the futon. "I know you can hear me right now, so I'm going say this once and for all. You thought I was six and didn't have a clue what you meant when you took this stone. You were wrong. I understood, and I secretly wished you had kept your promise. I was raised a sorceress— I'm not allowed to wish, to have hope, or to love. So I thought if I wished for your love and kept it a secret to myself, then my sorcery demon wouldn't know. So I kept it a secret. Through all those years when you hadn't yet found me, that was the only thing I hoped for. When you showed me the stone in London last month, I thought my secret hope had finally paid off. But I was wrong after all . . ." Tears streamed down her face now.

"I had been so wrong my whole life! You said you'd love me regardless of what I am. How noble of you. You don't think I can love you in the same way? Maybe the next thing you're going to say is that I want you for your money. But if you want to say so, you might have to shi—"

His mouth was on hers. He pushed her to the futon, his hands caressing every curve of her body while his mouth ravished her. He was starved for her. He'd shifted back to his human form in lightning speed. All six-foot-one of him wrapped around her long, lean body. He kissed, he fondled, he soothed, he wiped away the tears and the worries that dulled her eyes.

CHAPTER 31

The next day, Lorcan went for a run with Roy in their fox form. Roy taught Lorcan essential survival tips for controlling his shifting activities and how to utilize his were-abilities. After all, Lorcan was very new to the *were*-business. When the two foxes came back, Orla observed the magnificent sight of them. While Roy was large and quite bulky in the chest, he had short and shiny fur. His golden irises glowed. It seemed to her that he must have had some leopard in him—half-wolf, half-fox didn't quite explain his eyes. Lorcan looked more like a wolf than a fox with his long, glowing blue fur, especially around the face. His eyes were the same, striking blue. Both of them, Lorcan and Roy, were long, lean, and muscular, with the strength of predators. Seeing them, Orla made a mental note to never confuse were-creatures with ordinary pets—she could lose body parts that she desired to keep.

When the men came to the living room, fully dressed, Orla said, "I guess it's time for us to leave. Thanks for your hospitality."

Mori nodded. "I guess we part here. It was a pleasure meeting you."

Roy went to the kitchen to get himself a cup of tea. He sat down on the couch and said nothing.

"Very well then. Thank you again." Orla stood with Lorcan, about to leave.

"We can work together," Roy said and sipped his tea.

"Roy!" Mori sent Roy a disapproving look.

Roy shrugged. "That's what you told me. You said they could help by taking the key to somewhere safe."

"That was before what happened in the temple. Before . . . before . . ."

"Before Sai tried to rip your throat out . . . after he failed to kill you by tipping his wolves that you had been wounded by a bullet?"

Lorcan's eyes darkened. "You mean the bullet intended for me? I haven't had a chance to thank her for that yet. And you're saying someone was trying to kill her because she took that bullet?"

Roy leaned back in his chair. "There's nothing personal about her taking that bullet for you. She bit you without knowing you had were-blood. Your blood mixed, and you were both naturally bonded for a short period of time. The issue is that a dickhead in her clan, possibly a traitor, took the opportunity to send three wolves after her when she was injured."

"We don't have proof of that, Roy," said Mori.

"You speculated that yourself at the temple. Think about that, Mori. I know you think troubles follow you, but the truth is, we're stronger together. You can't go back to your clan."

"Why not?" Tears started to form in Mori's eyes.

Roy couldn't handle Mori's tears, and Orla knew they needed Roy to stay cool. Before he could utter insensitive words in response to Mori's tearful reaction, Orla jumped in. "But *we* need you, Mori. Really. We need your help. We need the key, or people will die, including us. We will protect the key because it's . . . it's our lives we're talking about . . ."

Lorcan sat down next to Orla and was about to say something, but Orla cut him off. "Roy, how do you think we could help? Come on, we need this."

Roy looked at Mori, waiting for a signal, then he said, "Sai was bought off by the Yakuz, Mori, and I'm afraid that the majority of senior members in your clan were, too." His voice was as cold as steel. Tears rolled down Mori's face now.

"At the temple, Sai gave you two options. He challenged you. If he won, he'd lead the clan and be in a position to access the key. If he lost, what did he promise you? It seemed to be fair at the time, right? If he lost, he'd spend the rest of his life guarding the key, meaning he'd know exactly where it is. Either way, it leads him directly to the key."

Mori sobbed, but Roy pressed on. "You were in the middle of it, so of course you couldn't see. But the other members of the clan were pushing you toward one of Sai's options. Think about it, Mori. I know it hurts. You love your clan, and you worked for it your whole life. You believe in it. But the Yakuz is the force of evil. You can't fight against it. I don't want to lose you, Mori."

Mori looked at Roy and nodded. Roy smiled, but it didn't last long. They suddenly heard the loud squawking of birds. Looking out the window, they saw a sky full of black hawks streaming at the house. There were similar to those that had attacked and killed the wizard—and they knew the old wizard had given Orla the map.

Orla darted toward her handbag which rested in a corner close to the door, but it was too late. The front line of the birds threw their bodies at the glass entrance as if on a suicide mission. The door shattered, and a cloud of black birds invaded the house. Roy pulled the cover from the sofa and wrapped Mori up, tightening his grip so she couldn't wriggle out. He drew his gun and shot at the birds with his free hand.

"Through the back door!" Roy yelled, dragging Mori out the back door with him. Lorcan grabbed his bag with one hand, and tried to protect Orla with the other. There wasn't much Orla could do from inside the house. They ran to the back yard, and once out in the open, Orla began to throw her fireballs. This time, the fire was lethal to the birds.

They ran toward Roy's car. He opened the front door and shoved the squirming Mori inside. He darted to the driver's seat while Lorcan and Orla jumped into the backseat. A few remaining birds hurled themselves at the car, but figuring they had no chance against metal, they flew away.

Roy drove away quickly.

"Where are we going?" Lorcan asked.

"To the key," Roy said briskly and focused his eyes on the road. Mori finally broke free from the sofa cover. She looked at Roy, and her voice was shaky. "You're scratched. Oh my God, you're scratched."

Roy shook his head. "It's okay."

But Orla knew it wasn't okay—she could see where the shoulder of his shirt was torn, the scratch marks had turned black. She swung her eyes to Lorcan and saw that the scratch marks on his arms and shoulders were bleeding, and the blood was red. "Are you okay, Lorcan?" she asked. Lorcan nodded, but he could see Roy's trouble as well.

"What is that, Mori?" Lorcan asked. Mori looked back at him, her eyes filled with tears already. "It's the Yakuz's poison. It's designed for were-creatures."

"Why didn't it affect me?"

Mori shook her head and said nothing more.

CHAPTER 32

Roy drove the car straight to the wooden dock. The wheels spun as he braked hard, and the car did a three-sixty and stopped with one wheel dangling over the edge. He pushed at the door, bolted out, and slumped to the ground. Roy was on his knees, breathing heavily. His eyes were dazed, and a stream of black blood trickled from of his mouth. Mori wrapped her arms around him, but he shrugged her off. He tried to yank at his shirt to pull it off, but Mori wouldn't loosen her grip.

"No," she said firmly. "You're not going to shift now. You're not going to die. You have to stay with me." He struggled again but couldn't loose himself from Mori's hold. "Get the boat, please," Mori directed Orla and Lorcan.

"Shouldn't we take him to the hospital?" Lorcan asked.

Mori shook her head. "It wouldn't help him. We have to get him to the temple, where the key is. It's a sacred place, it will heal him." Lorcan stared at her in disbelief, but as Orla rushed toward at the boat, he followed her.

"Do you really think that's best for him?" Lorcan asked.

"Mori knows best. We should take her word." She gestured at the boat. "It looks like you'll have to drive this beast. Ever driven a motorboat, smarty pants?"

"I'll look for the 'on' button," Lorcan said, letting Orla go to help Mori bring Roy to the boat.

***

Mori sat at the back of the boat, Roy in her arms. He was weakening by the second. In no time, they were sailing across the sea, Lorcan having figured out how to operate the boat. Roy shivered with the cold breeze. Mori gathered whatever she could find to keep him warm, but it didn't seem to help. His face had turned pale as a sheet, and his lips had blackened. She just gathered him into her arms and rocked, saying things in Japanese.

Orla didn't need Lorcan's translator to know Mori told him she loved him and he had to stay alive for her. It was all too familiar for Orla, the things a desperate and woman in love would say. But Orla wasn't sure Roy could hear any of it. Orla didn't realize, but tears were streaming down on her face. She felt the warmth of Lorcan's body when he wrapped his free arm around her shoulder, his other hand manning the steering wheel.

Roy opened his eyes and muttered something. Mori called out for Lorcan and Orla. Lorcan slowed the boat and rushed toward the back.

"Where you come from, is it a safe place?" Roy asked.

Many responses flashed through Lorcan's mind, but he simply nodded.

"Can you take Mori with you?"

Mori said something in Japanese—Orla knew she was begging Roy to stop saying things that sounded like his last words. But perhaps they were. Lorcan nodded again.

There was a loud bang on the side of the boat.

Lorcan thrust Orla behind him and moved toward the origin of the noise. At the front of the boat, he saw the whirlpool. In the center of the swirling water, an electric blue shape was surfacing. It had a long snout with fringe hanging from the bottom jaw, and it looked almost exactly like one of the ancient Japanese dragons he'd seen depicted in fairy tales. It had a serpentine build, and its head was large enough to swallow the boat whole. It stared at them, opening its enormous jaws wide, and shot a jet of water which hit the hull of the little boat with such force that it punched a hole in the bottom. That meant they'd soon be swimming. A second jet tore through the old wood. The third jet wasn't water, but looked like a pure bolt of lightning.

"We have to jump!" Lorcan said.

CHAPTER 33

Lorcan threw Roy overboard and jumped in after him. Mori and Orla followed. Roy sank like a stone, and he was too heavy for Mori to pull to the surface. Lorcan swam to her and grabbed Roy, floating to the surface with his unconscious body. The boat had not sunk yet, and it blocked their view of the monster. The group quietly tread water, moving silently toward something that looked like land in the distance.

When they looked back, they saw more lightning strike the boat, causing it to catch fire and explode. They swam for what seemed like hours to them, but finally came to a small island where they could drag their tired bodies from the water and flop in the sand. The sky in the direction from which they'd come looked inky black, illuminated here and there with lightning bolts.

Mori said nothing but scrambled toward Roy and performed CPR. Tears streaming down her face. There was no response from Roy. More wiped her tears and tried again.

It was too quiet.

Except the sound of water hitting the shore, they heard nothing else. But Mori wouldn't give up on Roy. She tried again.

A short time later, Roy spat out some water and took a deep breath. He was breathing, but barely.

Lorcan looked at both Mori and Roy. Orla knew he was furious at how hopeless their situation was. Then he pulled out his wrist unit.

"Oh my God, don't tell me it's damaged. It's our only way back to the Daimon Gate, Lorcan."

"It's fine. I'm going to call the Host for help. We don't have any other option, and we don't have time to explain to Mori about the multiverse. The dimensional travel and all that. The last thing we want is that she freaks out . . ." Orla raised her hand it stop Lorcan.

She turned and ran toward Mori, pointing behind her.

"Look out!" Orla shouted.

As soon as Mori turned to look and turned back, Orla landed a punch on the side of Mori's face, knocking her out cold. She turned back to Lorcan. "Does that help?"

He nodded and punched commands into his wrist unit while Orla dragged Mori toward a large stone, away from the wind.

After Lorcan had called, a beam of holocast appeared. Inside the beam was the hologram of the Host of the Daimon Gate, and he didn't look happy. "You're on a mission. It's inappropriate to directly contact me like this."

"I know, I'm sorry. But this is urgent, and we need your help. We're so close to getting the key. But the man lying there, he's been poisoned by those who stole it from you. He's the only one who has access to the key. We need to save him."

From the distance, in the dark, Orla raised an eyebrow as Lorcan lied right to the Host's face—without his usual obvious squirming. Most of the time, lying was her job.

"Lorcan, I'm not the right person to call on this matter for several reasons. I cannot help you regardless of how much I want to. The right person to contact is Ciaran."

"Ciaran! But how can I contact him? He's in another universe. Not only . . ."

"That's the only plausible way I know. I'm sorry. I have to go." The Host and the light beam of the holocast vanished.

CHAPTER 34

"**W**ait," Lorcan said helplessly, although he knew the Host could no longer hear him. Then he saw a small object lying on the sand. Lorcan picked it up and grinned at Orla. "Wicked old man," he muttered.

"Hush. What if he can hear you?"

Lorcan grinned again. In his hand was a wrist unit. It must be the communicator that connected directly to Ciaran. Lorcan entered the commands, and a holocast arrived, casting a circle of light in the sand. Inside it stood Ciaran LeBlanc, with a face that God had created when he was in a very good mood and the body of a warrior. Ciaran looked to be in a hurry, his hair tousled and his shirt unbuttoned. Ciaran was astonished to see Lorcan at the other end of the holocast.

"Lorcan?!"

Lorcan nodded.

"Do you realize you just hit the panic button of my private contact?"

"By private contact, do you mean your father?" Ciaran's eyes darkened, and Lorcan's requested more time to explain before Ciaran leaped out of the light beam and slit his throat. "The Host gave me the unit because I'm on a very important mission for him, and I need your help. He trusts me with the information about your relationship. You know the Host is not supposed to interfere with anything outside the Daimon Gate. He risked his life giving me this unit to contact you because he knows what I'm doing is important."

Ciaran stopped pacing. He nodded. "After the prank I pulled on my father, I deserve this."

Lorcan remembered vividly how Ciaran had tricked his father to get some information past the Daimon Gate's scanner. It was a big deal, and Ciaran felt remorse about it. The worst part was that Lorcan had helped Ciaran to carry it out. "Don't be too harsh on yourself. It wasn't exactly a prank. You needed the disc—it was important," Lorcan said. "Same with this now, Ciaran."

"All right. What do you need?"

"If you come a bit closer, you'll see a man lying in the sand. He's been poisoned." Lorcan walked toward Roy so Ciaran could follow him. The light beam circling on the sand around Ciaran shed enough light for him to see Roy.

"My father asked you to call me. Does that mean this guy couldn't be saved by any earthly means?"

"We're stranded on an island. He might not last long—even if I *could* get medical help here."

Ciaran nodded. "All right. I'll get my medical doctor. But he's never been to Earth before, and I can't risk him stepping outside the holocast. I'll have to bring your guy inside."

Lorcan nodded. "One more thing . . . Roy is a werefox. I think your doctor should be aware of that."

"I beg your pardon?"

"A werefox is . . ."

"I know what a werefox is . . . by superstition only. I can't believe you're using the term as if they exist in the real world . . ."

"Why would you say that?" Mori darted out from the dark toward Ciaran, followed by Orla, who was trying hold her back without success. "Please try to save Roy. We're werefoxes, yes, but we're not bad people."

"I didn't say that you were."

Mori shifted into her fox form, and then shifted back. "If you didn't believe, now you've seen it. Now you should believe. Please help him. Please."

Ciaran could see the devastation in Mori's eyes. He nodded and entered a command into his wrist unit. A tall young man in his thirties with blonde hair and an angelic face arrived. "Please step back," Ciaran said and then expanded the light circle. The two men approached Roy. The circle gradually grew wider until Roy was lying inside it under the bright light.

From the distance, Mori gasped. "They look so human. Beautiful."

Orla smiled. "I don't know about the doctor, but Ciaran *is* human. He's from London."

Inside the light circle, the doctor examined Roy, shook his head, and discussed something privately with Ciaran. The conversation seemed intense. Ciaran paced back and forth a bit, then came to the edge of the light and signaled Lorcan to come close to the light wall.

"I can't talk to the woman, Lorcan. Please ask her to stay over there." Lorcan turned around and saw Mori trying to move closer and Orla struggling to keep her away. Lorcan gestured for them to stay.

Lorcan put his hands into his pockets and spoke to Ciaran. "If you can't save him, just say it."

"It's up to you. I need your decision."

"Why me? Why not his woman?"

"She's too emotional. She'd agree to everything. You called me here. You're responsible for this, so you have to make the decision. Can you honestly tell me Roy is trustworthy?"

Lorcan realized he hadn't a clue. Their encounter had been too short for him to tell. Lorcan shook his head. "I don't know. We just met him. But he protects Mori—he loves his woman. And he took me into his home the day before yesterday, without even knowing me. I was in bad shape, and he kicked my ass just to shake me up. After an earlier attack, the poison was eating him up, but he still drove us to the dock. He knew he was going to die, but all he worried about was keeping Mori safe."

Ciaran nodded. "That's good enough for me. The doctor can't cleanse the poison already in his bloodstream, but the corrupted blood can be replaced with a clean substance."

"Substance?"

"Yes . . . kind of like a special type of blood. It has several good attributes, but the down side is that once we use it, we can't simply take it out and replace it with normal human blood. He'll be partially Eudaizian."

"It'll turn him into an alien?"

"Whatever you want to call it—it's just terminology. You live in the Daimon Gate, so technically you and Orla are aliens as well." Ciaran cocked an eyebrow.

Lorcan nodded and raked his hand though his hair. "Right, right. Sorry, I'm awfully confused right now. I guess the blood isn't the biggest issue here?"

Ciaran nodded. "Right. What I have to put into him is a secret substance only used for important people in Eudaiz. I'm in charge of more than six hundred billion citizens in Eudaiz, so I can't afford to risk anything when it comes to security. If Roy turns against us, if he gives a sample of this substance to our adversaries, I will have to kill him. Do you understand that? Can you relay that to his woman after this?"

Lorcan nodded.

"The substance is only sustainable in the Eudaiz environment, so he'll have to be our citizen. And as you know, we don't adopt people easily. If his woman isn't qualified, we might be able to take him only."

Lorcan shook his head and felt a pang of pain in his chest. This was all too familiar to him. It was the exact scenario he and Orla had faced when they were torn apart because of her family sorcery, and that was the reason he had entered the Daimon Gate. Lorcan knew he'd been lucky to cheat their way in, and now they were paying for that cheat. But what if Roy couldn't pull it off? That meant the decision made now would set them apart forever, should Roy survive.

"This should be Mori's decision." Lorcan shook his head.

"No, this should be Roy's decision, but he can't speak for himself right now. You called me here. I'm willing to risk our substance to save him. But the next part you will have to decide for him—and take complete responsibility if things go awry."

"Why does it have to come to this?" Lorcan raked his hair again.

"Welcome to my world. He hasn't much time. What do you say?"

Lorcan turned and looked at Mori. Then he turned back to Ciaran. "Do it."

Ciaran nodded at the doctor. The doctor pulled out a small box containing several pieces of compact medical equipment and crouched next to Roy. Ciaran was right next to him for assistance.

Ciaran knew the exact procedure. After the doctor injected something into Roy's arm, Ciaran held his body down when he tensed up and convulsed. He tilted Roy's head to the side so that he wouldn't choke when he vomited. Ciaran took his shirt off, wiped the black blood from Roy's mouth, and cushioned his head.

From a distance, Mori's eyes widened. "Is Ciaran a doctor?"

Orla shook her head. "Not really. But he has a wealth of knowledge, and he cares a lot for a great many people. He's a good man." Orla was thinking that she was glad she and Lorcan had decided not to betray Ciaran. She glanced at Lorcan, and when she saw him looking at her, she knew he was thinking the same thing.

Roy seemed to settle. Ciaran snapped a wrist unit on his right wrist and then came to the edge of the light. "What he has now is temporary," he said to Lorcan. "We will fully charge him in Eudaiz. The wrist unit must stay on him at all times, or he will die."

"How temporary?"

"I'd give it a week. As for you, never use that button again. Return the unit to my father. If you ever need to contact me, this one is yours." Ciaran put another wrist unit on the sand. He turned to signal the doctor it was time to leave.

"Wait," Lorcan said. "Brandon attacked us in the Daimon gate and wanted us to expose your activity to the council. We didn't. Your father knows about it now. I thought I'd let you know."

"Brandon? Prince of the Red castle?"

Lorcan nodded.

Ciaran rolled his eyes and shook his head. "All right, I'll handle that. Thanks." Then Ciaran, the doctor, and the light beam vanished.

CHAPTER 35

When the sun came up at the horizon of the magnificent sea, Roy stirred and awoke. Mori gathered him into her arms and burst into tears. "A magical man came and saved you."

"Well, it wasn't exactly magic. The work Ciaran and the doctor did was completely scientific. How do you feel, Roy?" Lorcan asked

"I feel like I could move a mountain." Roy stood. He was six feet tall, but at the moment, he seemed to grow two inches taller, and he was glowing with energy and virility.

"You look well," Orla said.

"I should ask Ciaran for some of the substance for myself!" Lorcan muttered. Then he whispered into Orla's ear about Roy's one-week lifespan. Orla squealed and walked away, waving her arms in frustration.

Lorcan looked at Roy and Mori. "She didn't like my joke," he hastily explained as he scurried after Orla.

When Lorcan caught up with her, Orla lowered her voice so Roy and Mori wouldn't hear. "One week? How are you going to explain that to him? How are you going to tell Mori?"

"I didn't have a choice. Plus, he won't exactly die within a week—but he does have to go to Eudaiz. As long as he's alive, we can sort things out, right? Let's try to look at this in a positive light, shall we?" Orla contemplated and then nodded.

They returned to Roy and Mori at the beach. Lorcan spent some time discussing the wrist unit with Roy, letting him know how important it was to keep it on at all time. He gave Roy a sketchy description about what had been done to save him, but he withheld the information about one-week life span on Earth. Roy seemed to be open enough to accept whatever information Lorcan offered.

Once Roy's briefing was finished, Orla moved on impatiently. "Now that the stupid birds have the map, we've got to hurry to get to the key before they do. We need your help on that. How long is it going to take to find the key?"

"It's not far away—just over there." Mori pointed to a strip of land floating close to the horizon.

Lorcan squinted as he looked to where she pointed. "Right, let me just call in a chopper," he said sarcastically.

"Really?" Roy asked.

"No, not really. I don't have access to resources like that." Lorcan rolled his eyes.

"Then how are we going to get there?" Orla asked.

"We'll have to swim," Roy responded.

Mori dove head first into the cold water. She swam like a fish. Roy followed. Lorcan rumbled and dove in at Orla's push. Not much later, they'd reached the stretch of land Mori had showed them. It had looked farther than it actually was. As they gathered on the dry sandy beach, Mori glanced around, and her eyes clouded. "They're here. The Yakuz are here already."

"Where is the key, exactly?" Orla asked.

"In a temple on top of the hill. I have guard foxes permanently placed there, but I'm not sure how many men or creatures the Yakuz have brought with them, or what kind of weapons they have."

"We were chased out of the house. We've got nothing to fight with. Even Roy doesn't have his gun now," Lorcan said.

Orla and Lorcan looked toward the interior of the island. In front of them was a gigantic hill of sand. The coastline curved away, and they couldn't see the other end unless they went around the hill. Bleached white sand carpeted the entire area, black rocks hopping up here and there. Sand as far as the eye could see.

"What are the Yakuz anyway? Mysterious creatures? Criminals? We've run into all forms on them since we came, and everyone has referred to them with fear, and with one word—Yakuz," Lorcan muttered.

"They majority of them are human outlaws. But they have a lot of money, so they hire creatures with magical talents and abilities, including were-creatures, witches, wizards, sorcerers, you name it. If any magical forces have reached the high ranks of the Yakuz, I don't know about it. And whether any other groups have enough power to hire the Yakuz to do their bidding, I have no clue," Roy said.

The four of them walked slowly around the sand dune. Mori signaled everyone to hide in the shadow of a large rock. Via a gap, they could see large groups of furry black wolves pacing.

"Werewolves?" Lorcan asked.

"Too far away to tell, and too many of them to go ahead on," Roy said.

"Werewolves or not, let's see how they do against hard shells." Orla rushed back to the water, Lorcan at her heel. A slow smile curved her luscious lips as she dipped her hands into the water.

"What's your plan, Orla? I don't like surprises."

"They have their minions, and we should have ours." She stretched her hand out into the water. Small jolts of purple lightning danced from her fingertips out into the waves. Small granules of sand began to swirl around her fingers.

She was forming crabs out of sand. They began to scuttle around on the bottom of the sea. She made their color more substantial, bright red, and then sent small bolts of lightning into them, forcing them away from the island to grow rapidly to roughly the size of a man before coming back.

Mori and Roy approached, and Orla grinned as she gestured toward the sea. The red claws of an army of crabs slowly crept out of the water and headed up the hill to where the wolves kept watch. It was show time. From behind the rock, they soon heard the howls of wounded wolves echoing out from the other end of the sand hills. Peeking through the gap again, they saw the bodies of wolves scattering the sand field and the red-claw army retreating back to the sea.

"The entrance of the temple is right on top of the hill, facing east. Once inside, I can show you where the key is. My foxes should be guarding all the way up to the entrance of the temple," Mori said.

"It's more than a hundred yards from here to the bottom of the hill. And then we have to fight our way up. Do you have any idea how many there are on the other side of the hill?" Lorcan asked.

"I'll go and take a look," Roy said.

"No, Roy. You're not going in by yourself."

There was a low growl behind them, and they slowly turned around. Six wolves approached the, teeth bared. Roy, Mori, and Lorcan immediately shifted into their fox forms. The trio was magnificent in blue, black, and red. The fight broke out and soon became a flurry of flying sand. Lorcan took on as many as he could to keep wolves from attacking Orla.

In this world of were-animals, Orla felt a bit out of place. She looked over to the rock, strategizing a way to approach the temple gate.

CHAPTER 36

The trio had knocked down the attack wolves with ease, but the noise they'd made may have alerted the Yakuz at the top of the hill. There was no way they could make it to the sand hill and then fight their way up. Orla tried to recall all the lessons and practice she had received during her short training in Ireland.

She closed her eyes and willed herself to summon the dark force. She knew Lorcan wouldn't approve of this, but she had no other option. She crouched and braced her hands on the cold sand.

Power, she needed the dark power. She started chanting. Gradually, she could feel it rising inside her. Waves of fire energy stormed into her like a tsunami. She felt as if she could move mountains, drain oceans, and draw up wild storms.

Orla stood, her eyes blank, her body and hands glowing with magical light. The foxes had won their battle and shifted back to human form. Lorcan saw Orla, and it instantly registered what she had done. He ran to her, and she stared right through him. She raised her arms, sending lightning bolts streaking across the blackened sky and smashing into the entrance of the temple. Thousands of bolts struck all the way down the hill. The trees on the hillside caught fire, and Yakuz bodies and body parts flew into the air.

Orla heard Lorcan call out to her from somewhere amid the noise and destruction, but she couldn't stop. Nature's attack kept crashing into the hillside until not a sign or sound of live creatures echoed their way. Orla's eyes were completely blank, and her long black hair trailed in the wind, the air whirling into eddies of freezing air when she lifted her arms.

"Shall we go!" she whispered into the wind and raised her arms, palms up, singing a strange chant. The ground underneath their feet rolled in waves, curved up and surged into a gigantic sand wave, carrying the four of them right to the shattered entrance of the temple.

Once on the ground again, Orla's arms flopped down to her sides as if the power was exiting her body. Her eyes came back to normal. Lorcan knew too well what would happen next, and he dashed toward her to catch her before she fell head first onto the stone floor.

"Orla, Orla, honey, come back to me, please." He had seen her use magic, he had seen her sending people—including himself—to Hell and back, but he had never seen her work with such magnitude. He wasn't sure she could come back from this at all. If he lost her here and now, the whole ordeal wouldn't mean a damn thing to him. But shortly, she stirred and opened her eyes. Lorcan squeezed her into his arms. "Oh God. Please don't do that to me, ever again. Promise me? Please?"

She smiled groggily and nodded.

Roy and Mori came back after a quick search around the outside of the temple. "They killed all of my guard foxes." Tears swam in Mori eyes, and Roy hugged her tightly.

"You couldn't have known. If anything, I bet this is Sai's doing," he said.

Lorcan helped Orla up. "Can you walk?" She nodded.

They cautiously pushed what was left of the temple door open. The last piece of wood crumbed as Roy touched it. The temple was eerily quiet.

"The key is at the far end." Mori entered through the doorway, intending to lead the group, but Roy pushed her behind him. They had only gone a few yards when a string of men cut off the corridor. Lorcan swore under his breath and stood in front of Orla.

She rolled her eyes. "I can fight, Lorcan. At least this is men on men. We're a level playing field now."

Lorcan glanced at Roy, who was ready for a fight. "You take the back row, I'll take the front row, and we'll meet in the middle when we're done." Lorcan's voice was casual, and he didn't seem worried at all.

Roy gave him a curt nod, then began walking toward his appointed gaggle of goons, trying to draw them out one at a time. Orla turned and sauntered toward the other end of the corridor where she found a few men lurking. She kept one hand behind her back as she walked toward them, carefully and stealthily building a ball of purple lightning in her palm. She paused in front of the middle person and smiled. Six feet still separated them, but she was close enough.

"I'm going to go out on a limb here and say that there's no way that we can work this out civilly?" she asked sweetly. Silence met her question, and she could feel herself getting more irritated. Finally, in answer, the line of warriors took on a fighting pose, ready to attack. She refused to be intimidated. Sneaking her other hand behind her back to make a second ball of energy, she watched and waited. The first attack came from the far left. There were five of them, but the one on the end leapt into action, spinning a katana above his head as he began a complicated dance to move closer to her. Orla threw a ball of energy at him, and he was engulfed and lifted into the air until he hung about fifty feet above the ground. Even as the panic showed in his face, he didn't make a sound. The bubble disappeared, dropping him back to the hard-packed earth of the floor. Orla waited with baited breath, but he didn't move again.

The second ball of energy easily dispatched the next attacker in the same manner as the first, and she turned to the three that were left. All three of them were advancing on her, weapons out. That put her at a distinct disadvantage. The first guy lunged at her with a katana, and she managed to squeak by without harm. The second one had nun chucks, and he was moving quickly toward her, swinging them in an impressive pattern. Orla reached her hand out, lightning fast, trying to grab one of them to wrest it away from him, but she only succeeded in getting a wallop on her hand that made her think she'd gotten a broken bone in return.

"Okay, Little Miss Nice Girl is gone." Her snarl came out of nowhere, and it was enough to make the third one hesitate a bit. He had a crude bow and arrow that she thought wasn't going to do him any good fighting in such close quarters. She sent a bolt of energy at it and watched as the weapon disintegrated in his hands. He looked up at her incredulously, and she pretended to blow smoke off her fingers like she'd just fired a gun. They stared at each other for a while, but then the enemy turned and ran.

CHAPTER 37

Orla came back to the main entrance and saw that everyone had gathered there. Lorcan glared at her and said nothing. She knew he was mad because she'd sneaked behind his back and went in for a fight. But it was done now. She merely smiled in response to his scowl.

Seeing the tension between them, Mori smiled. "Glad to see you came back to join the party."

Orla sneered. "Not much of a party for the goons."

Roy chuckled and pushed at Lorcan's elbow. "Come on, we have a key to fetch. Cheer up!" Lorcan mumbled something and shuffled along the corridor.

"Lorcan, do you know where you're going?" Mori asked.

He shook his head, then stopped and waited for the group to catch up with him. "I'm sorry about your foxes," Lorcan said to Mori.

"Don't worry. It couldn't be helped. If we can just get the key and put it in a safe place, perhaps that will give these foxes peace—and justice."

"Then who will give *you* justice, Mori?" Sai's voice exploded from the right corridor. They turned and looked down the hall but found no sign of him. Lorcan had thought the voice and the echo were a bit odd, so instead of looking toward the right, he looked to the left, thinking the sound had perhaps bounced from the left in the opposite direction. He was right. From the left corridor, Sai charged out with a gun in his hand, aiming straight at Mori. Lorcan had enough time to push her aside, but he took the bullet in his shoulder.

Without losing a second, Roy charged at Sai, grabbing a metal candleholder on his way. Before Sai could register Roy's movement, Roy had whacked the gun out of his hand. Roy pounded on Sai, who was at a great disadvantage in size, strength, intelligence, and willpower. After a good

215

pummeling to his attacker, Roy let Sai flop to the floor, but as soon as Roy turned his back, Sai surged up, knife in hand. Mori yelped. Quick as lightning, Roy turned back, landed a final blow on Sai's face, grabbed his hand, and turned his own knife on him. In a flash, the knife sank up to the hilt into Sai's chest.

Lorcan was on his knees now, and Orla was holding him. The pain was bad, but he said nothing and willed himself not to pass out. He grabbed at the floor for purchase and breathed heavily. Roy crouched. "You have to let go. You have to pass out or your body won't start healing. I told you, Lorcan. Our healing processes are all different. That's how your body works. Just lie down, right here. We'll guard you."

Lorcan's eyes were blurry. He flopped to the floor, but pushed up again. "There's no time for it. We're in the middle of this. I can't lie down. We don't know what else might be coming." He stood. And then they heard a muffled cry for help. The sound was very familiar.

"Chiyo," Orla said. They searched the area and found Chiyo tied up and blindfolded in a dark room at the end of the corridor. When they entered the room, Chiyo withdrew, "Who are you? Don't touch me. Please don't beat me. I don't know anything."

"It's us. We'll get you out of here." Orla took the blindfold off. As soon as Chiyo saw Lorcan and Orla, tears streamed down her face. Orla untied Chiyo. She wore the same clothes she had worn when they captured her at the warehouse. Her wrists were marked with bruises and dried blood. Her hair was tousled. Lorcan helped her up and let her cling onto him, although he could barely stand by himself.

"We should go get the key and find a safe place to stay tonight," Roy said.

Mori nodded in agreement and led the way. They wound their way along another long corridor that ended at a double door leading to the main part of the temple. As Mori opened it, a beautiful woman stood in front of them, smiling. Mori moved back and hissed. Roy muttered loud enough for everyone to hear, "Hina, the virgin princess of the Yakuz."

The woman was nearly naked, wearing only the sheerest of long, gossamer robes. She looked more like a sex symbol than a virgin, Orla thought.

"Welcome to my temple," she said. "You must be Roy, the mixed-blood hero. And you two are the travelers from a faraway land." She nodded at Lorcan and Orla. Her voice was as clear as a bell.

"This is not your temple," Mori growled.

The woman smiled. "You must be Mori."

Hina had advanced slightly toward Mori when Roy snarled, "One more step, and I will cut your throat out."

Hina stopped and withdrew. "You need not fear me . . ." But before she had finished the sentence, her right arm shot out like a snake, flew over the thirty feet of distance between her and Mori, and grabbed Mori's neck, pulling her over like a rag doll. She pulled Mori close against her body, her fingers at Mori's neck now morphed into five sharp steel blades.

"I'm going to have to borrow her for a bit. Please excuse us." She pulled Mori out the door and into another corridor.

CHAPTER 38

The group followed to the other room. Roy's eyes were bloodshot. Hina didn't stop them from following.

"She needs Mori to pull the key. She's the chosen one," Roy growled as he followed Hina and Mori. He picked up a knife lying on the floor next to a dead body.

Hina's eyes glowed with insanity the closer they got to the key. They entered the main chamber. At the far end of the room was a raised platform which looked like some kind of monument. There was a golden padlock on it, and a gigantic golden key fixed inside. Hina dragged Mori toward the platform. She pushed her face at the key.

"Draw the key out and give it to me."

Her fingers cut into Mori's neck, and streams of blood flowed out, but Mori stood still.

"Pull the key!" the princess roared.

At her back, Orla's hands curved into fists as she began to form fireballs. But reading her thoughts, Lorcan grabbed at her hands and shook his head.

"Give me the key." Hina tightened her grip. More rivulets of blood ran down Mori's neck.

"Give it to her, Mori, please," Roy begged.

Mori nodded slightly and raised her right hand slowly, and as soon as she touched the key, it glowed in recognition. She turned the key three times until it clicked and pulled the key out of the lock. As soon as she had removed it, she used her left hand to grab Hina's right wrist so she couldn't swing and slice through her throat with her blade fingers. Still holding the key in her right hand, she shoved it into Hina's eyes. Hina roared, staggered back, and loosened her grip on Mori's neck. Seizing the opportunity, Mori freed herself.

Seeing Mori was out of the danger zone, Roy charged at Hina. Before he could reach her, Orla had sent a fireball right at her. She fell but managed to throw her snake arm out, slashing at Roy. He fell to the floor. Mori was furious. She picked up Roy's knife, threw the key toward Lorcan, and flew at Hina. Dazed by the strike from Orla's fire, Hina didn't react quickly enough to avoid Mori's knife. It pierced the woman's heart, and she dropped dead before she could speak another word.

Mori rushed over to Roy. "Roy, talk to me." Roy moaned and got up. "I'll heal." Mori wrapped her arms around his waist to help him up. Orla checked on Hina to ensure that she really was dead. They heard Lorcan grunt, and he rolled back into the room, lying on the floor with a fresh gash on his arm. Outside the door, Chiyo stood with the key in her hand. She punched a button at the door, and the steel bar doors fell down, blocking ways out to all corridors.

"Why, Chiyo?" Lorcan asked.

The woman smiled. "Chiyo was sacrificed for my God a long time ago. I have lived in her skin and have been waiting for this for a long time. I'd almost lost hope before you two came along." She looked at Lorcan and Orla. "I haven't thanked you yet for that. If you hadn't stirred this up, I wouldn't have gotten this far, and the Yakuz would have gotten the key by now. We deserve the key much more than the Yakuz."

"*We?* Who are *we?*" Mori was furious. She grabbed the barred door and shook it fiercely, but it wouldn't budge.

"I'm sorry but your Fire Fox clan is doomed and gone," the woman said and turned on her heel, disappearing down the end of the hallway.

The entire building shuddered. "It's going down. The temple is going down," Roy said. Everyone searched for a way out, but all exits had been barred. The temple shook, and dust from the ceiling and loose objects started falling to the ground. Lorcan and Roy ran to a storm drain at the corner of the room and lifted the lid. Roy climbed down first. Hopping back up, he said, "It's okay. Come down." He helped Mori and Orla down, and Lorcan slid down the hole just before a stone column collapsed right on the spot.

They followed the drainage system until it opened up into a tunnel. They ran in the dark as fast as they could. For a while, they'd seen a glimpse of light at the end of the tunnel. Finally reaching it, they bolted out the other side of the sand hill. They looked up to the top of the hill, watching as the temple crumbled, caved in, and collapsed. Dust and smoke formed enormous balls which hovered in the air, their shadows looming over the sand island.

At the far end of the curved sandy beach, they saw the woman they knew as Chiyo removing her clothes in a ceremonial manner and walking toward the sea with the key in her hand. On the horizon, the dragon creature that had attacked their boat surfaced and raised its head high above the water. The sky around it darkened and storm clouds gathered.

Mori and Roy sprinted toward the woman. Orla ran after them. Lorcan was staggering, his wounds bleeding badly. He slumped to the sand, shaking his head and trying to stay alert. Orla returned to Lorcan, but he waved her away.

"They need you. Help them." As Orla ran toward Roy and Mori, Lorcan reeled toward the bodies of guard werewolves they had killed before.

The woman had entered the water and was walking out to the open sea. The water was at knee level, and soon she would be swimming toward the dragon. Mori bit her hand and tried to yank the key out. Roy sprung up from the water to land on the woman's shoulder, intending to bite her throat. The dragon slung a water jet at Roy, deflecting him before he could get to the woman. Roy dropped into the water. The woman screamed and cried at the same time, she tried to shrug Mori off so she could swim toward the dragon. It appeared as if the dragon couldn't strike Mori as he would have to hit the woman as well.

Orla curved a fireball in her hand and threw it at the woman. It had just left the tips of her fingers when the dragon shot a hard spray of water at her. Orla fell onto the sand, skidding away several feet. Her fireball flopped to the water and fizzled.

The woman had disentangled herself from Mori, and Mori dropped to the water. She could see the dragon aiming in her general direction. As the woman turned again toward the open sea, Lorcan darted out from the sand hill will a knife he had found on one of the guard wolves. He threw it at the woman. The knife spun in the air and then stabbed into her from the behind, plunging into her heart. She turned toward Lorcan, and he could see the life draining from her eyes. Lorcan looked at his hand in disbelief—he had never thrown a knife in his life.

Mori pulled the key from the woman's hand as she fell into the water and paddled safely back to land. Roy also returned. In the distance, the dragon's strident roar seemed enough to crack the ozone layer of the Earth. It turned to glare at the four on the beach.

One look at the dragon, and Orla knew disaster was imminent. She yelled out to Mori and Roy. "Come inland! Quickly!"

CHAPTER 39

Under the blackened sky, the dragon had raised up fifty feet in the air. Its eyes glowed with a blood red fury. Orla knew it was conjuring a tidal wave. Mori and Roy had reached her, and Lorcan approached from behind. Orla turned toward them, yelling, "Get back, get back, give me some space!" She looked at the dragon, concentrated, raised her arms, and her eyes once again went blank.

Mountains of water rushed in toward the shore, enough to swallow the entire island. Orla chanted her spells. In opposition to the dragon's rough seas, she was as calm as still water. She didn't rush, didn't panic. Lorcan stood right behind her, flanked by Mori and Roy. If they were to die on this island, they'd die together, fighting as one. As Orla chanted, the sand moved. They could feel the ground grumbling. The island shook. Orla raised her arms again, uttering a command that was completely foreign to Lorcan.

The tidal wave came close to the shore. It was so enormous that it blocked their view of the dragon. Similarly, the dragon couldn't see them. The sand surged up in the air like a row of skyscrapers or an army of gigantic sand soldiers. In a flash, before any of them could register anything, the sand met the water. The giant wave broke and shattered, and sank back into the ocean. The dragon roared his protest and vanished.

Lorcan ran to Orla, thinking she would collapse. But she turned around and looked at him gently, saying, "I'm okay. It wasn't the dark magic that I used. I'll thank the late wizard later. But now, we need a shelter. The dragon will return soon, and I'm running out of resources."

They hid behind a large rock on the beach. "We can't risk swimming back to the mainland. Water gives us nothing but a disadvantage at the moment," Roy said.

"It'll swallow the island on the second attack," Orla said, flopping into the sand. Lorcan sat, leaning against the rock, his eyes rolling back and his vision blurry.

"You have to let your wounds heal, Lorcan," Mori said.

Orla reached over to pull him into her arms. "Come on, lie down here."

Lorcan raised his arm to stop her. "I can't. We have to get out of here." He pulled out his wrist unit and started to program it. His hands shook, and his vision got worse by the second.

In the distance, they heard the low growling sound of the dragon coming back.

"Roy and Mori, we came from the Daimon Gate, a universe far from here. Orla and I can go back via our portal, but I'm not sure how it works with you. The Daimon Gate doesn't accept uninvited guests. If we violate any rule there, you'll die . . ." Lorcan had to stop speaking to take a breath. "So I'm programming it so that we only get to the transitional zone. Then I'll go into the Daimon Gate and seek permission to take you in."

"It sounds like a reasonable plan," Roy said.

Lorcan shook his head, more to stay alert than in response to Roy. "The transitional zone is nobody's land. No one is in charge, and no one governs it. You could be attacked by any number of creatures while waiting for me. That's the risk, if you're willing to take it."

"How likely is it that we'd be attacked?" Mori asked.

"I don't know. I've never been."

"I'll risk it. I'll go with you. How about you, Roy?" Mori asked.

"I don't have a better alternative. Any place is better than in the stomach of that thing." Roy pointed.

Lorcan cursed under his breath and turned back to the unit to finish the program. Soon, a ring of light appeared inland, and their portal opened. It was two hundred yards away, and they had to run across an open sand field. Lorcan lay back on the sand, on the verge of passing out.

"You go," he mumbled, closing his eyes.

"No, no! Look at me, Lorcan." Orla shook his shoulders, but he wouldn't open his eyes.

Mori dragged Orla away from Lorcan. Roy kicked a pile of sand right into Lorcan's face. Lorcan grabbed at his face and grumbled.

"That'll wake you. You wouldn't let yourself pass out when I asked you to . . . but now is *not* the time," Roy growled, hooking Lorcan's arm over his shoulders and hoisting him to his feet.

The group raced toward the open portal. The dragon saw them go and hurled as much wind and water as it could toward the group.

They jumped into the ring of light, and the light withdrew and vanished. From above, they got a last glimpse of the island as it was swallowed by the dragon's tidal wave.

The transitional zone was as dark as the tunnel in the island had been. "I don't know where we are. It's not supposed to be a tunnel," Lorcan said. They kept running, searching for some light. Lorcan pulled out the unit Ciaran had given him and punched the alarm button. The group kept moving forward. Freezing wind blew through the tunnel, drawing them toward the far end. At the side of the tunnel, a beam of light flashed on, and the door of a spaceship opened.

"Thank you, Ciaran," Lorcan said and ran to the door. They all jumped in, the door closed, and the ship lifted off, hovering and then zooming away smoothly. Lorcan slumped to the floor of the spaceship and finally passed out.

A while later, Lorcan opened his eyes, finding Orla smiling at him. He was snuggled comfortably in her arms. "How are you?" she asked and kissed him.

"Perfect." He smiled up at her. "How did you beat that dragon without dark magic?"

"The late wizard told me to utilize my talents, remember? My talents don't lie in dark magic. I have an extended family, and some of my relatives are white witches. They taught me all sort of things. I can conjure up astrological elements to serve whatever purpose I want. The water element is what the dragon used, and earth is the element that destroys water."

Lorcan chuckled. "Indeed."

"I missed your blue fur. Can I rub it, just once?"

He stopped smiling.

"Too soon?" Orla pouted.

Lorcan rolled his eyes. Then Orla saw her blue fox looking at her with puppy eyes. She grinned, burying her face into his long fur, but then got his mouth instead. He had shifted back.

"That's cheating," Orla said but continued to kiss him. Afterward, Lorcan rolled to his side and saw Mori and Roy seated stiffly on the floor across the spaceship. Lorcan chuckled.

"Can you tell us where we're going?" Roy asked.

Alarm bells rang in Lorcan's head, and he realized it was time to tell Roy about his new blood and the deal with Ciaran. Lorcan sat up.

"This is Ciaran's spaceship, so I'm guessing we're going straight to Eudaiz. I've never been there, so I can't tell you much, but from what I've heard, it's a heaven, a universe of beautiful and happy people. It's a universe of true happiness."

"A universe?" Mori raised an eyebrow.

"Well, just like our Earth, our world, there are many universes that exist that we haven't visited," Lorcan responded.

"Alien?"

Lorcan shook his head. "As long as you're not talking about the green aliens you often see on TV, I can live with the term. It's a very long story. But you'll see it for yourself."

"So I'll have a chance to thank Ciaran for saving me. It's good to hear there's a place where true happiness exists," Roy said.

Orla rolled her eyes. "Try a universe of virtue," she muttered, thinking of the Daimon Gate.

"I'm sorry?" Roy asked.

"Don't worry about it. The less you know, the happier you'll be," Orla said.

"Humm." Lorcan ruffled his hair.

"What? Why don't you just spit it out? I can take it." Roy raised his voice.

Lorcan cleared his throat. "Right. Here's the thing. Ciaran couldn't cleanse the poison from your system, so he had to replace part of your blood by a substance only available in Eudaiz. It's no big deal, really. You can become a Eudaiz citizen and receive the supply for the rest of your life. Ciaran owed us a favor, and he's willing to take you in because of that. He's a very fair man. But he doesn't necessarily have to take Mori."

"And what the fuck does that mean?" Roy growled.

"Ciaran doesn't know you. He's responsible for a lot of people, and it's difficult to take in random strangers. Having said that, once he gets to know you, I don't think it will be a problem. But you have to be patient. We can't expect to go there and have them lay out the red carpet for us immediately." Lorcan kept his voice as low and calm as possible.

"What would the worst scenario be?" Mori asked.

"That would be going back to Earth to be eaten by that dragon monster," Orla answered.

The spaceship seemed to have come to a stop and was now hovering. Lorcan stood, hauling Orla up with him. "We're here!" Lorcan exclaimed.

As the door slid open, a robotic voice spoke, "Welcome to Xiilok. You have arrived at the residence of Prince Brandon."

"What the fuck?" Lorcan yelled, "Wait!" to stop Roy and Mori from reaching the door.

"Close the door, close the door!" Orla shouted.

Roy pushed the door closed. The spaceship shuddered, and the lights were cut off.

The group stood in darkness.

CHAPTER 40

They struggled in the cabin of the spaceship for what seemed like decades. Except for the sound of the machinery clicking and humming, there was no other sound in the dark that was recognizable. Lorcan knew that in a few seconds, their enemies— whoever or whatever they were— would break in, and that might be the end of them. He concentrated. *Where did he go wrong?* They were on Earth, they were being attacked, he had opened the portal so that they could travel to the transitional zone in between the universes. Lorcan braced his hands against the control panel in the dark and probed for the buttons. The lights had been cut off as well as the energy. The air would be the next thing to run out. Lorcan raked his hands through his hair, retracing every step again from the beginning, from when they first escaped the Dragon's attack to when they ended up wherever they were at the moment. He couldn't figure out what he had done wrong.

The spaceship was hovering now, and the creatures out there could roll it over any moment. The sounds of footsteps, claws, and hard objects hitting the outside of the spaceship echoed inside, making every nerve in his head throb. *They were not going to die here,* Lorcan thought. He wouldn't let anything happen to Orla, or his friends.

Whatever was out there was shaking the spaceship now, it had to be very big and strong, and there would be many more of them around. Hand-to-hand combat was not a wise solution at the moment. They had to stay put inside the cabin.

But the air was getting thinner by the second. Every breath they drew could be the last one.

Nobody said anything, which made things worse as the creatures' roars and squeaks outside became more prominent and haunting.

Lorcan's hand hit a square button. All the other buttons were round, but this one was square. He bit his lips, pressed the button, and prayed that it was not the one that opened the door automatically.

It was not.

Instead, a dim light lit up in the corner of the spaceship's cabin. Lorcan turned around. He could see now. Mori and Orla held the doors together to keep the creatures outside. Roy helped from the middle, pushing the handles of the two doors tightly together. All three were pale and exhausted, and they looked ready to give up any second.

The spaceship was shaken again, tilting left and right, up and down.

"I'm going to get this thing moving," Lorcan said.

"Hurry, Lorcan!" Orla exclaimed.

"If memory serves me right, this is my very first time operating a spaceship. It's most likely a lot more difficult than you think," Lorcan said in frustration as he typed a series of commands into the control panel. The spaceship jerked, lifted, swung a bit, and then moved backward. The movements were so jerky that everyone thrown to the floor. "Great, we're going backwards, but at least we're moving."

They were moving backward at an incredible speed.

"Do you know where we're going?" Roy asked.

"The place where the spaceship was taking us was obviously wrong. I'm trying to un-go, if it's at all possible," Lorcan mumbled. "Maybe we could . . ." But before Lorcan could finish his sentence, the spaceship hit a hard object from the behind, the wall caved in, and the spaceship started to dive. Lorcan grabbed at the control handle, and pulled. In response, the spaceship stopped diving. Lorcan entered a landing command, and prayed that it worked. It did, and they landed. Before they could say anything, the electrical wires sparked into fire. "Get out!" Lorcan yelled.

Everyone dove from the spaceship, just a split second before it exploded. They crawled on the ground, trying to get back on their feet. When they stood, they could just make out a small army of creatures in the distance, approaching them and brandishing weapons, claws, and foreign objects that weren't recognizable to them.

"Holy shit," Roy said.

There was no way that they could fight, especially when they didn't have any weapons. Just then, from behind them, they heard a male voice say, "Get down."

They dropped to the ground, without question or hesitation. A small spaceship came to a stop behind them, and from inside it, black laser beams sliced through the air, slaughtering the space creatures and obliterating the army. The group stood and turned around to see who had saved them. From the small spaceship, Ciaran LeBlanc stepped out, a formidable presence with the aura of a dark angel. He holstered two laser guns and approached the group.

"Does the king of Eudaiz normally engage in combat alone?" Lorcan asked.

"No, I have soldiers and armies of people working for me when it comes to engaging in real combat, both on Earth and in Eudaiz. But I consider saving idiots to be my personal problem, and for that I spared my people the chase. You hit the panic button to call for my help, but you had left the position before my people arrived. Do you know how dangerous it is for me to send my soldiers to the transitional zone? If I hadn't jumped on my personal spaceship and followed my instincts, you'd probably be tucked cozily in those creatures' stomachs by now," Ciaran fumed.

"We ran into a tunnel, and then that was the only spaceship we saw, so we jumped on. Then it went in the wrong direction. We didn't have a choice," Roy said.

"Whose spaceship was that?" Orla asked.

"I thought it were one of yours," Lorcan explained.

Ciaran looked at the spaceship, at the moment no more than a pile of scrap metal, with disdain. "I don't know, it's not qualified to be called a spaceship, and it's certainly isn't mine," he said.

"The spaceship sent us to Xiilok and Brandon's residence. It seems Brandon has taken residence in Xiilok, and he's out of the control of the Daimon Gate," Lorcan said.

Ciaran shook his head. "Brandon would rather be an outlaw of all the universes than be a minor gatekeeper in the Daimon Gate. It takes all kinds."

Roy staggered a bit and walked toward the corner, leaning against the wall. Mori asked, "Are you okay?"

Roy tried to respond to her question, but his body had a mind of its own, and his eyes rolled up before he slumped to the ground.

Mori grabbed him. "What's happening to him?" she asked.

Ciaran quickly checked the wrist unit on Roy's right wrist, and he said, "He's out of energy. I gave him seven days' worth of energy, but because you took him traveling across multiple dimensions and across the transitional zone, his energy level has been depleted."

"Can you give him more?" Orla asked.

"Yes, but it's only temporary. I have to get him to Eudaiz ASAP." Ciaran took a small square black patch from his belt and snapped it into the wrist unit that Roy was wearing. The glowing green light of the level indicator on the wrist unit lit up. "This is very temporary. And again, because we have to cross dimensions of time and space, I don't know how long it'll last. He has to go with me now. Whatever you need to do with the Daimon Gate, you will have to do it without him."

"All right then," Lorcan confirmed.

Roy opened his eyes and sat up. He had heard the last thing Ciaran said. "What about Mori?" Roy asked.

"She'll have to go with Lorcan. I can't take her to Eudaiz now. I haven't discussed it with my council," Ciaran said.

Roy stood and walked away. "I can't leave Mori."

"I gave you the energy, but I can take it back at any time. It's your choice." Ciaran's patience had run out.

"Look, Roy, this is temporary. Go with Ciaran now to get yourself fixed up, then we can reunite later. I'll get a guest pass for Mori at the Daimon Gate. You're both going to be fine," Lorcan said.

"If we hang around here any longer, and the creatures come back, we'll all be dead. It's not just about you," Orla snarled.

At the back, another small spaceship arrived and parked. A couple of uniformed officers stepped out and approached Ciaran. Ciaran nodded in acknowledgement. "My officers will take you to the entrance of the Daimon Gate. Roy, what's your decision? If you go with them, you'll die in a few minutes," Ciaran said.

"Roy, please go with Ciaran. We'll meet again soon," Mori said.

Roy nodded reluctantly. Mori, Lorcan, and Orla entered the newly-arrived spaceship. Ciaran waited until it had departed safely before he took Roy into his ship. Once inside, Ciaran verified himself using his left palm and activated the machine. It hovered smoothly and then swiftly darted into the holo-space. "Destination, Eudaiz, Sciphil Zone, Tower Three." Ciaran gave a verbal command. After the computer acknowledged the destination, he turned, about to ask Roy something, but his wrist unit flashed a signal. Ciaran glanced at the information on the small screen, then looked at Roy.

"What did you try to do for the Host of the Daimon Gate?"

"We tried to get the key of Psuche to the Daimon Gate for safekeeping."

Ciaran nodded. "And that required a fight with some sort of creature at sea?"

Roy nodded.

"You killed it?"

"We barely escaped with our lives."

Ciaran cocked an eyebrow.

"It's a dragon, as big as a mountain. How would you expect us to kill it?" Roy asked in frustration.

Ciaran shook his head and gave a verbal command to the machine. "Change destination, entrance of the Daimon Gate. Engage holocast communication with the Host of the Daimon Gate immediately."

SPECTRUM OF LIES
BOOK 3

CHEAT A SORCERER
-INDIGO STONE -

CHAPTER 1

Heat. That was all he could feel. A wave of fire that carried incinerating heat was flying toward him. Lorcan stared at it as if it was a movie clip shown in slow motion. Once that fire brushed over him, Lorcan knew all that would be left of him was a pile of ashes. He was stuck beneath a collapsed brick dome, half of his body was buried, and his legs were crushed. He didn't think there were any bones left intact, so even if the bricks and stones didn't crumble down upon him, he wouldn't be able to move out of the way of the fire anyway.

As death loomed close, he thought of Orla. He hadn't had a chance to marry her properly. He thought of his family in Ireland, too, and regretted taking their love for granted. If there were a God—and somehow that God was compassionate enough to grant him another chance—he would take Orla to Ireland to meet his family and marry her. On top of that, he would go to church every week.

Brandon's laughter still echoed in the air—the sound of evil. *How could a gatekeeper in a virtuous place such as the Daimon Gate turn dark so quickly?* Lorcan wondered. As he closed his eyes, awaiting the coming fire, he heard the sound of a spaceship moving closer. Turning toward the noise, he saw it had parked close to where he lay. From inside the spaceship, Ciaran jumped out and rushed over to Lorcan.

"Go away! There won't be enough time, Ciaran!" Lorcan yelled. *That man must have nerves of steel,* Lorcan thought. Without a word, Ciaran blasted his weapon at the loose bricks around Lorcan and then used his daggers as levers to lift the large stone from on top of Lorcan. Ignoring Lorcan's verbal abuse, Ciaran hauled Lorcan up and half-carried, half-dragged Lorcan into his spaceship.

The door closed and sealed immediately after their embarkation.

"Heat defense mechanism on!" Ciaran shouted. The spaceship shuddered, and they heard a click.

"Affirmative and ready," a robotic voice said.

Then the storm of fire hit them.

The spaceship tilted slightly when hit, but regained its balance soon after. As the counterbalance mechanism kicked in to compensate for the heat outside, the air inside the spaceship dropped to freezing. The storm continued to attack the spaceship from the outside. They heard the sound of hard objects hitting metal, and the force of the air blew through gaps in the outer body of the ship, creating a hellish howling noise.

Then it quieted down, the fire went past, and the spaceship seemed to settle.

Lying on the floor, Lorcan's vision became blurry. He knew he needed to pass out so that his body could begin the healing process, but he had to tell Ciaran about his healing ability first or he would think that his system was collapsing. *"Damn it,"* Lorcan thought. He couldn't force a word past his lips. And as he'd predicted, Ciaran was trying to prevent him from passing out because in the same situation, a normal person would pass out and go into cardiac arrest due to the shock of the injuries and the extreme changes of environmental conditions they had just experienced.

"Lorcan, come on. Open your eyes for me. You're not going to die on me. Come on." Ciaran shook Lorcan's shoulders so hard that there was no way he would be able to pass out and start any healing process. Lorcan wanted to scream, but again, he couldn't get any words out. Ciaran ran to a small compartment and pulled out an emergency medical kit. Lorcan opened his eyes and saw Ciaran preparing a syringe. It had to be adrenaline, Lorcan thought, which normally he wouldn't mind, but if that kick-ass chemical was injected into his system now, he'd be forced to remain conscious and deal with this excruciating pain.

Lorcan summoned all the strength he had left and said, "No."

Ciaran cocked an eyebrow. "No? It's only adrenaline. I know what I'm doing."

"No," Lorcan repeated, but Ciaran approached him, still ignoring his weak protest. Ciaran crouched next to Lorcan, but before he could inject the adrenaline, something hit the spaceship so hard that it almost tipped the craft over. Ciaran fell, dropping the syringe on the floor, and it rolled away to a far corner. He hurried toward a control window to look outside, mumbling some profanity as he went.

On the floor, Lorcan took his opportunity and slipped into his needed unconsciousness.

After a while, Lorcan opened his eyes to find himself alone, lying on the floor of the spaceship. His body had healed. Getting up, he went to the window to see what was going on outside. A short distance away, Ciaran and a group of soldiers had barricaded themselves behind the ruins of a gothic dome and were firing at a small army of space creatures. To protect Lorcan, Ciaran shot and killed any creatures veering toward the space vessel.

Lorcan immediately recognized the ambush attempt that had caught him off guard before. He searched the spaceship for the weapon compartment. He grabbed two long laser beam guns. He'd never used them before, but in looking them over, it didn't take him long to figure out where the triggers were. Unfortunately, as soon as he touched the handles of the guns, a line of text flashed on a small screen located above the trigger: *Unauthorized User*. Lorcan swore and ran to the control panel. He slammed his palm on the verification screen and, ignoring the machine's protest, hacked into the system. It didn't take him long to prompt the system to give him a pass for weapon usage. Lorcan scanned the receiver of the gun over the verification screen dashboard and the recognition mechanism on the gun flashed a green light.

Outside, Ciaran had nearly wiped out the small army, still keeping an eye on the spaceship to be sure no stray creatures wandered near it. He felt a sudden blast of heat and dust pressure coming from behind, an area that, oddly, backed up to a dead end wall of rock and stone. Ciaran was sure that nothing could penetrate the wall to come out at him from that corner. But it then dawned on him that he was fighting at a transitional zone in between universes. The dead end could be merely an illusion, and a dimensional hole could open before he had a chance to react. He whirled around to face the general direction from which the blast had come, but it seemed to be too late. He shouted to his soldiers to take cover and dove behind a rock.

The pressure came like an explosion. He and all of his soldiers were thrown feet away, tossed around like rag dolls. Dazed, Ciaran tried to sit up and see through the dust storm. He saw nothing but the shape of a man walking toward him. He groped for his weapons on the ground nearby but found nothing but dust. He could feel the warmth of his blood streaming out from a gash on his left shoulder. Ciaran tried to spring to his feet, but his body wouldn't obey. Looking up, he saw Brandon standing right in front of him, a cold smirk on his face.

"Never thought you would face death like this, did you, Ciaran?"

CHAPTER 2

Ciaran looked at Brandon in the eye. "Why? I saved your life."

"Well, you should have asked me if I wanted that. You think you know it all, Ciaran? You, the Host, and those stupid humans are trying to obtain what doesn't belong to you."

"The key of Psuche? What does it have to do with you?"

"I could take the time explain to you why you must die today, but I'm not feeling compassionate at the moment. So goodbye, Ciaran LeBlanc, king of

Eudaiz. You will die on the battlefield like a common soldier."

Brandon raised his crossbow, aiming at Ciaran's head, but Ciaran swung his leg and kicked the weapon away. His second kick landed on Brandon's abdomen, sending him staggering back and falling to the ground. Still groggy, Ciaran struggled to his feet and was then assaulted by Brandon's two-leg kick. He skidded backwards and fell back to the ground. As Brandon stood up and ran to recover his weapon, two streams of laser beams blasted at his chest. His clothes became engulfed in flame, but he pulled a lever and the fire died out instantly. Brandon released a black smokeball and fled the scene.

Lorcan hurried into the dome of dust and black smoke to drag Ciaran out.

"I've got this! Let go!" Ciaran shrugged off Lorcan's support and walked out of the dust on his own. He inhaled some clean air and coughed out the dust that coated this throat and lungs, recovering swiftly. Then Ciaran turned around, looking at Lorcan. "Are you okay?"

"Yes." Lorcan grinned.

"Did you know the best way to kill a creature in space is to aim at the head? You're using two laser beamers, and all you did was set Brandon's clothes on fire!" Ciaran exclaimed.

"I've never used these before, so that's good enough, isn't it? I didn't miss totally!"

"Brandon ran away—again," Ciaran mumbled, clutching his bleeding shoulder. He glanced around, taking stock of the situation. "And he killed seven of my best soldiers."

"Shouldn't you be relieved he didn't kill you, too?"

Ciaran said nothing and headed back to his spaceship. Lorcan followed, and Ciaran asked, "How can you walk like that now? A short while ago, you were dying."

"I knew that would be the first thing you'd ask when you saw me! I wasn't dying. I have the ability to heal myself, heal my injuries very quickly, but I have to shut my system down first."

They were inside the spaceship now. "You can heal yourself?"

Lorcan nodded. "Yes, as long as I haven't died, I can heal myself from injuries. To what extent, I don't know. It's all new to me, too."

"Right." Ciaran rolled his eyes.

"Ciaran, I know it's hard for you to accept anything you can't explain scientifically. It was hard for me, too. But when your life partner, the person you've spent your entire life with, tells you she's a sorceress, you kinda learn to accept things that seem a little beyond reality."

Ciaran nodded. "Are there any more special abilities you and your group have that I should know about?"

"Apart from what you already know—Roy and Mori are werefoxes, and Orla is a sorceress—nothing else. Anyway, why are you here? I thought you were taking Roy to Eudaiz."

Ciaran shook his head. "I got a message on way to Eudaiz with Roy. I came back for you, and the girls said you'd gone. What happened?"

"I was on my way to the Daimon Gate to get the guest pass for Mori. Brandon ambushed me exactly the way he did you just now. He thought I had the key with me, and when he couldn't find it, he left me buried in the ruins and went after Orla. We have to get to her."

Ciaran shook his head. "I've sent for her. They'll be here soon." He glanced at his wrist unit. "My officers just confirmed. They're safe and sound."

The sound of an incoming holocast interrupted, and a beam of light flashed inside the spaceship, inside of which stood the life-sized hologram image of the Host of the Daimon Gate.

"You're injured, Ciaran?" the Host asked.

Lorcan nodded, acknowledging the Host. The Host responded in turn.

Ciaran winced and walked toward the medical compartment. He pulled out a square medical patch and cleaned his wound. "I don't have the ability to heal myself quickly, but this will help clean things up. It should look better by the time my wife sees it." Ciaran flashed Lorcan a brief smile and then addressed the Host. "I called for you because one of the missions you sent people to complete on Earth might have caused collateral effects that I don't think you'll be happy about. I placed our intelligence system on Earth to keep an eye on things, and the system has just reported that a sea creature is gathering a massive amount of energy under the seabeds of all continents on Earth. That amount of energy could create a series of tsunamis."

Ciaran looked straight into the Host's eyes. "It's going to drown the entire human population. This creature has something to do with the Daimon Gate. What can you tell us about the key and the mission you ordered?"

The Host arched an eyebrow and stared at Ciaran. Ciaran shrugged. "I can certainly find out myself, but it will take precious time that we might need in order to save the humans on Earth. I still have interests on Earth, so I'd like to protect the people there," Ciaran explained.

The Host nodded. "There was a myth before my time that the key of Psuche can give the holder the ability to control the water level of any universe, given the correct lineup of all astronomical elements. For me, it's simply a key to secure one of our Eastern gates."

Ciaran nodded. "For creatures that live in an aquatic environment, water dictates their territories and is a prime motivation for invasion."

"I killed the woman who was supposed to give the key to the creature. It looked quite pissed. I'm not sure if it was because of the woman's death or because it couldn't get the key. But whatever the reason, if we go back to Earth to kill that reptile, do you think it would solve the tsunami threat?" Lorcan asked.

Ciaran nodded. "It's speculation, but it's better than doing nothing."

Lorcan pulled out a little pouch and put it on the floor. "Here is the key. I'll leave it with you, and we'll return to Earth for the creature." He looked at the Host.

Ciaran arched an eyebrow. "I thought you said you didn't have it with you?"

"I'd hidden it before Brandon attacked me. Just got it back now."

"Brandon?" the Host asked.

Ciaran nodded. "He was trying to kill me, too. He's taken residence in Xiilok, outside your jurisdiction. And now he—or the person who took him in—wants the key, too. Maybe the myth has some truth to it—perhaps the key of Psuche does have magical powers," Ciaran mumbled sarcastically. The Host stepped forward, moving the light beam up to encircle the pouch on the ground. He then bent down to pick it up.

"Oh, no." The Host shook his head.

Lorcan and Ciaran watched the Host as he pulled out the key and pointed to its top. "The stone is missing. There's an Indigo Stone that's supposed to be mounted right here."

"So the key won't work without the stone?" Lorcan asked.

The Host shook his head. "The stone carries the power, and the key unlocks the power. They won't work separately. This is now simply a metal key, and the stone an expensive decoration."

"But we took the key out of the patch lock at the temple. My guess is that it had to have the stone attached to it at the time— the Fire Fox clan wouldn't have spent generations and sacrificed many lives to guard a useless key with no power. And the woman grabbed the key from me and ran to the beach. It wasn't long before we caught up with her, and we killed her before she could give the key to the dragon. So what happened to the stone in between?" Lorcan exclaimed.

"Time is relative," Ciaran contemplated.

"How does that explain any of this?" Lorcan raked his hands through his hair and paced in agitation.

"Did anything strange happen between the time the woman took the key and when you killed her?" Ciaran asked.

"Not really. She locked us in the temple and triggered a mechanism so the temple collapsed, and we were buried. We escaped via the drainage system beneath the temple. The only thing that was strange to me was the drainage. It was like a tunnel—long, dark, and confusing . . ." Lorcan trailed of as a thought came across his mind. "Dimensional hole . . . do you think that's what it was, Ciaran?"

Ciaran smiled and nodded. "The woman was obviously going to give the dragon the key without the stone. There must be more to that woman than meets the eye."

Lorcan rolled his eyes. "Yeah, she stripped naked on the beach."

"I beg your pardon?" the Host asked.

Ciaran laughed. "Never mind," Lorcan rumbled and continued, "So I guess we leave the key with you here and go back to Earth for the stone and the dragon?"

Ciaran nodded. "You might be able to kill two birds with one mission. Take these." Ciaran removed handguns from the weapon compartment and programmed them. "These are specially designed for the transitional zone, so I think they'll work on Earth. They'll definitely be superior compared to the current technology there and won't be detected by any detecting device." Ciaran gave Lorcan the guns. While Lorcan assessed the weight and the feel of them, the Host shook his head.

Ciaran merely smiled at the Host and muttered, "I'm sorry your peace-keeping mission isn't working out. But my friends are still on Earth. I'm not going to let them die because of this stupid reptile."

CHAPTER 3

Hot sand rubbed at her face. Orla rolled to her side, moaning. Her entire body ached, but it was not the pain of battle, it was the pain of overtaxed body muscles after a body combat session at the gym. She opened her eyes, squinted at the bright sunlight, and immediately recalled what had just happened. She jumped to her feet, searching for Lorcan.

Behind a small sand hill, Lorcan drew himself up, squinted his eyes groggily, and registered the situation. He swung around, catching sight of Orla, and grinned. "Are you okay?" he asked, glancing up and down her body.

Orla nodded. "You?" She turned him around, checking him over.

"I'm fine."

From behind a small shrub on their left, Roy and Mori stood up, taking inventory.

"How are you guys?" Orla asked.

"We're fine," Mori responded.

Lorcan ran back to the sand hill where he had landed and dug around in the sand. When Orla, Roy, and Mori approached, Lorcan explained, "I'm looking for my wrist unit."

"The one Ciaran gave you?" Orla asked.

Lorcan grunted a response and breathed a sigh of relief as he saw a black band sticking up from the sand a few feet away from him. Picking it up, he brushed the sand from it with the sleeve of his shirt. After blowing off the last bit of sand, he started coding. Everyone's eyes were on the device, the only tool they had at the moment to reopen the portal that would take them back to the transitional zone of the multiverse. The device flashed green, signaling that it was operational. Lorcan sighed a breath of relief and put the device away.

Orla rubbed at her shoulders. "It was a rough landing, wasn't it? I thought Ciaran was more skillful than that when he opened the portal for us."

Lorcan smiled. He came over to massage Orla's aching shoulders. "He is skillful. You should see him in battle. The transition was bumpy because we ran into some dust storms along the way. Anyway, I hope there won't be too many rough days ahead of us."

Orla rolled her eyes. "We can only hope."

Roy stood stiffly, looking at Mori. "We'll be all right. We'll find the stone, and then return to the transitional zone. I'll take you to Eudaiz."

"Is that what Ciaran promised?" Mori asked, arching an eyebrow.

"If we complete this task, Ciaran will take you in. You can trust him—he's that kind of guy," Lorcan said.

"And you know that because . . . ?" Mori asked.

"We've had a lot of dealings with Ciaran. He has more important things to worry than dishonoring his promise," Orla said.

Mori shrugged.

"He saved me and asked nothing in return, remember, Mori?" Roy asked. Mori looked at Roy. There was so much more she wanted to say to him, but she couldn't say it in front of Lorcan and Orla. She tugged at the new weapon Ciaran had just given them to make sure it was secured, then walked away. "Where are we?" Roy asked.

"Ciaran showed me the map of the energy moments underneath the seabeds, but we didn't have a chance to convert the information to a surface map. But I think we're somewhere between Japan and some small islands in Southeast Asia. I could locate us by triangulating the wrist unit and the base station, but I'm reluctant to activate the signals unless it's absolutely necessary. We can ask the locals." Lorcan squinted, his hands on his hips, and glanced around the endless expanse of white sand.

"Well, this looks very promising," Orla said, rolling her eyes. From the corner of her eyes, she saw a small head with black hair popping in and out from behind a black rock. Without a single word, her hand was on her weapon, and she was charging toward the possible stalker. She moved too fast for the person behind the rock to react or run away. The group followed her.

Orla pulled her gun, pointing it at the rock. "Come out and raise your hands where I can see them." For Lorcan, she added, "Yes, I learned that from cop shows on TV."

From behind the rock, a small child stepped out. He was a boy about ten years old with short black hair and huge brown eyes, which were filled with tears. The boy had his hands in the air, suggesting he'd understood what Orla said.

"Hey, don't worry. I'm not going to shoot you," Orla soothed. She almost sounded like she was singing a lullaby. She put the gun away. The boy put his hands down, but his eyes still gleamed with tears. "I'm sorry I scared you. It's okay now. We won't hurt you. We're just a little bit lost. Do you know where we are?"

The boy stopped shaking, and a faint smile came across his face. Lorcan approached and pulled out the liquid map Ciaran had given him previously. He programmed it to reveal the surface map of the Earth and zoomed in on Asia. "Do you think you can point out on the map where we are now?" He laid the map on the ground where it flattened out and expanded like a paper map. Lorcan made a mental note to praise this technology to Ciaran. The boy crouched next to the map and reached his hand out, pointing to a particular location on the map, but before his finger could make contact, he turned his hand and pulled the gun holstered on Orla's belt. The boy jumped back to his feet, stepped back, and held the gun shakily in his little hands, pointing it at the group of people.

"Easy, easy, kid, that's not a toy," Lorcan said.

"If you put it down, and go away, we won't chase you. We don't mean any harm," Orla said.

The boy's eyes fixed on Roy and Mori. He stepped back as the group advanced. Then he lifted the gun, pointed it at Roy, and pulled the trigger. Mori yelped and dove at Roy, squashing him down.

For a limited time, D.N. Leo gives away
4 books in the Multiverse Collection

CLAIM YOUR FREE E-BOOKS
http://narrativeland.com

THANK YOU FOR READING!
D.N. LEO

D.N. LEO 'S NOVELS
SERIES READING ORDER

http://narrativeland.com/dnleonovels

—

A SHADE OF MIND
(narrativeland.com/shade)
Main Characters: Ciaran, Madeline, Tadgh, and Jo
(Recommended reading in order)
1-4 Random Psychic
2-4 Forever Mortal
3-4 Elusive Beings
4-4 Imperfect Divine

—

SPECTRUM
(narrativeland.com/spectrum)
Main characters: Lorcan, Orla, Roy and Mori
(Recommended reading in order)
1-4 White Curse
2-4 Blue Fox
3-4 Indigo Stone
4-4 Red Moon

—

MINDSCAPE
(narrativeland.com/mind)
Main characters:
Ciaran, Madeline, Tadgh, Jo, Kyle, Hoyt, Ayana, Pete, Sizx, Lorcan, Orla
(Recommended reading in order within series, can be read in ANY order in related to other series)

Queen's Gambit
Knight & Pawn
Lone Castle
Doubled Bishops
Dead Squares
King's Endgame

—

SILVER BLOOD
Main characters:
(narrativeland.com/silver)
Ciaran, Madeline, Tadgh, Jo, Caedmon, Sedna, Roy, Mori, Zach, Mya, Lorcan and Orla
This series can be read in ANY order within the series and in related to other series.

Virgo
Libra
Scorpio
Taurus
Pisces
Gemini

Thank you for reading.

If you enjoyed reading **Spectrum of Lies – Book 2**, I would appreciate it if you would help others enjoy this book, too.

Recommend it. Please help other readers find this book by recommending it to friends, readers' groups and discussion boards.

Review it. Please tell other readers why you liked this book by reviewing it wherever you purchase the book from. If you do write a review, please send me an email at info@dnleo.com so I can thank you with a personal email.

COPYRIGHT

BEFRIEND A ROGUE
-BLUE FOX-

SPECTRUM OF LIES
BOOK 2

By D.N. Leo

www.ingramcontent.com/pod-product-compliance
Lightning Source LLC
Chambersburg PA
CBHW060624260626
47161CB00008B/2796